Beata Rustica

The Tale of the Would-Be Saint

Books by Meredith Steinbach

Novels:

Beata Rustica: The Tale of the Would-Be Saint

*The Charmed Life of Flowers:
Field Notes from Provence*

The Birth of the World as We Know It; or, Teiresias

Zara

Here Lies the Water

Short Fiction Collection:

Reliable Light

Beata Rustica
THE TALE OF THE WOULD-BE SAINT

A Novel by
MEREDITH STEINBACH

HOUSE OF REMINGTON
PUBLISHING

Copyright © 2013 by Meredith Steinbach

All rights reserved.

Published in the United States by House of Remington Publishing, Bristol, Rhode Island. No part of this book may be used or reproduced in any manner whatsoever without written permission from the publisher. For information, contact House of Remington Publishing, P.O. Box 1045, Bristol, Rhode Island 02809.

ISBN: 978-0-9882836-1-9

Designer: Mary Tiegreen
Cover painting: "Astrea" by Nicholas Harper

This is a work of fiction. Any resemblance to real places or persons, living or dead, is purely coincidental.

Printed in the United States

For B.G.,
who taught so well
the significance of the very small

With gratitude to Fran O'Donnell and
Benny Lichtner for tireless attention to
detail and support

And with continuing gratitude to
Mary Tiegreen for her exacting eye,
her exquisite artistry, and her delight in
the very nearly impossible

"I had an excellent seat and delicious refreshments were served to the ladies between Mass and the execution."

—*Candide*, Voltaire

I

And so finally it was evening. The sun fell like a tortured yolk into the frying pan. The family could see it from the kitchen as they sat around the table, barefooted and dumfounded, jawing at one another, throwing the one kitchen towel back and forth to wipe the chicken grease from their chins. As always, Beatrice lay in the dwarfish cradle beside the fan, in the same bassinet her father had made for her birth nineteen years before in the Distant Territory. Now on the hottest day of the year, she had refused again to eat. As she lay carefully counting the beads of her tiny necklace, she looked out over the edge of her basket at her so-called family and thought—not without a little sadness—how unfortunate it was that she herself had become the false droplet tainting her family's stream.

That morning Beatrice had weighed in at twenty-seven pounds when the Immense Grandmère placed her in the baby scales, three pounds less than the day before. It was an impossible rate to keep up, but none-the-less, at the end of the eighth day, if she could keep up such a rate, there would be only three pounds left to oblivion. What, she was wondering, would it take—exactly—to be named a saint? And so, she wrote it down directly in her Book of Dreams lest she forget this question during her self-imposed rituals of passage, and so that on the issue of sainthood the documentation might help later on, in presenting her case.

To outsiders, all the village people, and the local animals, too, seemed to have shrunken into a diminutive state—no matter that Beatrice was the singular, unusually short person in the territory's known history. Even the county map now said in finely italicized red letters:

ELVES

next to the dot and the black lettering of the village name.

Tourists thought Beatrice already to be a saint, while the villagers openly stated that soon enough, as the fast went on, she would be declared one. The rumor of her approaching sainthood was also fueled by the fact that many of the villagers had read in the encyclopedias on sale in the local grocery that elves were not much for living lengthy lives. It was written that would-be saints by committing a profound sacrifice—such as by starving oneself to death—might be immortalized. Already Beatrice had a following, which met regularly next to her bedside table.

Yes indeed, the villagers whispered: Yes, indeed. To live so close to a trace element brought one a nearly imperturbable peace. And, they said, who could shrug shoulders at Imperturbable Peace? In their quest for consolation, they could not get close enough to Beatrice when she offered guidance to visitors in the afternoons from one to three.

ON THE SIXTH DAY

Nomenclature

So far she had been called Dwarf, Runt, Peewee-Elfkins, Nainette, Hobgoblin Bobgob, Whichermathingy, Punk Pitikins, The Pet's Pet, Teeny Deevil, Scrumpchdidliumptious—during an unfortunate if temporary falling out—Hairless Wonder, Amoeba Girl, and Microcosmic Mimi by members of her own family. By those who called on her, she had been revered as Saint Intrepid Angel, Our Tiny Deliverer, Miniature with Imaginary Wings—and so forth. She had no reason to doubt that Beatrice had always been her given name, but for her own purposes she had chosen to shorten it to B. in her Book of Dreams. If she fasted long enough, she considered, she might extend her names, starting with the one she had been given, which she considered an appropriate one for a saint as it had already been used by one. There was a certain comfort in names, all names. Some people had been fortunate enough to have received many names at birth, so she had heard; but so far as she knew, even counting the possibilities of reincarnation, she had not been one of them.

Her mother had been opposed to naming rites, and therefore her grandmother had named her and said a few secret words over her at the sink, blessing her and asking mercy and guidance for her in her life. And, it was her grandmother who stood most aggrieved at the girl's insistence upon an approach to sainthood in part by way of withholding food.

No matter that many had predicted her immediate demise, Beatrice figured that the elfin life might yet turn out to be a long one after all. At least one of her philosophical heroes had lasted forty days in fasting without ill effect—if one discounted subsequent crucifixion. She herself had fasted six days and five nights, and it was the sixth night upcoming, so far without a vision and only with inconsequential distress. She had lost no further weight. Just the same, she was thinking, who could believe what had happened in one's own life, much less in what anyone else had had to endure, in any century?

SEVENTH DAY

Leanings

Until she'd come along, theirs had not been a religious family. In their secular roots, her father was a hamster farmer; but once, he had been an administrative official in the Distant Territories and a reliable teacher of an advanced form of arithmetic. Her mother, too, was a hamster farmer, by virtue of being married to one, though her mother and Beatrice herself had never had the occasion to go anywhere near a hamster. The Beautiful Mother persevered to the admiration of the villagers nearly all of every day, over the Scrabble board in the corner of the two-story cottage, decrying everything about the current government as Beatrice's visitors passed by. Although it was to hamsters they attached their reputations, for their livelihood they looked to grain. In a descending series of calamities, their family had raised up and sawn off crops of soy, wheat, corn and rice—and in the year of the Hundred Year's Flood, barley, sunflowers, and sorghum.

Although Thin Grandpère had been a political figure in the national government, neither he nor Grandmère minded sharing their experiences with a primordial dwarf, or reading aloud for hours, even with a kindly tone—much to her own Beautiful Mother's embarrassment and distaste.

Her twin brothers Beatrice merely looked upon with tolerance: there at the table in their wrecked jeans, their bare feet like clumps of dough on the floor beneath the round oak table where they ate. Bare-chested, somewhat hairy, awkward, smelly—so she suspected by the sweat beading on their arms—the two of them together resembled a giant, two-headed, sunburnt octopus. To a young adult gnome in a basket, having one younger brother who was a tease might have been unfortunate, but on top of it she was having to manage double brothers, without prospect of escape. There were many misfortunes in her life, she realized while falling into self-pity from time to time. Having twins for younger brothers was more than one of them. When she raised her head off the pillow and contemplated sitting up, their catcalls sent her head into a vertigo that was in itself reasonably deafening. She rested her head again. Always she kept her irrational, hostile thoughts to herself—but for a few sour comments to her sympathetic grandmother. In her humble opinion, she told Grandmère, The Twins were nothing but irreversible, deviant sloths. It was a bother to think about them for any length of time. It had occurred to her in the night that perhaps her younger brothers ought to be reformed. If not in a state reformatory, then she heartily recommended, as soon as possible they might be declawed. Her grandmother styled a guffaw. This was often Beatrice's way—to suffer in near silence, concocting endless imaginary scenarios. She cleared her throat. Helpless, she lay in her crib, prevaricating. I am lost and alien in my own family, she thought. I am nineteen. What is the meaning of life? I am not microscopic! Nor imaginary! she exclaimed. This is my actual life! Sacrosanct as anyone's! Too real! The sound of brotherly chewing filled the room.

ON DAY EIGHT

Contemplations

A foray to the Distant Territories by her parents had neatly circumscribed her birth and was rarely, if ever, mentioned by the family. She was the only villager in her age group to have been born outside Central Territory. This, in itself, was seen by village historians as something of an accomplishment. She remembered the return trip and planned someday to record it in the Book of Dreams. Her life was rather dreamlike anyway, viewing the world as she did from the crib.

Someday, she hoped, she would jot more than notes in a particularly enthusiastic plan for the pygmy life. On other days, she was sure she would write only for her own amusement. Some passages would be an expression of what she called Beatrice's State of Grace. But for now, she knew and was not afraid to say to herself once again: This dwarf is truly in a darkened frame of mind.

It was said by her faultless grandmother that malnutrition might precede such a truncated state of mind as was hers and that there was an immediate remedy for it—if only, if only, she would relent a little and partake, if only of this little fruit cup or this crepe filled with luscious chocolate and hazelnut paste.

.

ON THE NINTH

Pop-bead Philosophy

It was pleasant to look into each pearl on Beatrice's necklace where the plastic had begun to peel off into her pop-bead philosophies. There she could not see herself but she could imagine it almost as though it were the very first time she had laid eyes on her face. A lovely young lady she was, with a deep-set stare—very dark blue almost grey. Everything about her was in proportion to every other thing. Around the edges reflected in the bead were her pleasing pitchy black curls, almost blue—for there was a fretwork of premature silver weaving its way throughout Beatrice's tresses. She had seen it threaded through her brush when her grandmother combed her hair back onto the pillow in the bed, unless of course it had been some of Grandmère's own. She could not be sure. They had always had clean hair, and always the family would take a certain pride in it—so her grandmother encouraged every day.

But, would hers always be washed in a basin, in this very bed? This, Beatrice asked herself repeatedly. This, she entered into her mental notes most carefully. It gave her a crick in the neck just to think of it, and also the creeping feeling of a little imagined moisture running down her spine.

Grandmère fondly said more than once that her granddaughter's imagination would get her into extraordinary trouble one day.

"Good," Beatrice laughed. "This dwarf'll be on the lookout for it," she said. "Send a little trouble my way."

"Never tempt fate like that!" Grandmère admonished, rather sternly, to which unusual harsh tone Beatrice looked up in dismay. She was lying on her stomach just then, reading a book on the effectiveness of using mere pinpoints to remedy ills in a practice most foreign to her indeed. Grandmère laughed then to ease her pain and swiftly and very gently swatted Beatrice's arm.

It was very hard to lie in a crib for the entirety of one's life. It had a tendency to make the joints ache, and there was absolutely, as far as Beatrice could see now, nothing for it but acupuncture. This surely might be a way, she thought, into the new dwarf life and atmosphere.

"No wildness now," the so-called elfish grandmother—who was nearly six feet tall any way you looked at it and just as wide—said as she tried to spoon in some broth past a tinkling diminution of teeth.

"I am just one very wild coyote you see right here, lounging about before your eyes," Beatrice winked.

And then, she heard The Beautiful Mother's cold laugh echoing: "Wild coyotes! Pah! Wild coyotes, such as the likes of you, living in laminated wicker baskets! You might as well be stuffed." The Beautiful Mother laughed then so hard she coughed, and then she coughed so hard she laughed again and several scrabble pieces moved far out of place.

The rest of the family—all but Grandmère who had had the pleasure of giving The Beautiful Mother birth—joined in laughing, chortling in agreement, as they always did whenever The Beautiful Mother said anything she thought might amuse.

Grandmère exchanged a long sad glance with her little charge while across the room the dishtowel flew around the dining table like a poorly destined bird from chin to chin, a practice that so disgusted grandmother and granddaughter alike, both to no earthly end.

ON DAY TEN

A Good View

Now in Beatrice's Book of Dreams and only there, at the age of eighteen Beatrice had worn glasses. In her life, she had never worn glasses, but she had always wanted them as her vision troubled her. Grandmère had lent her Grandpère's lenses, though Beatrice could only thereafter see with one eye closed. Then, after a time she couldn't remember which eye was the good, which the bad. Squinting through one eye and then the other, she had gone about in her basket until somehow by accident she had managed to step on both the crystal lenses—in her tiny dream.

One moment both lenses lay beside the bed untouched in their little gold wire frames. In the next, her unremedied sight, as well as the excruciating sound of Grandpère's glasses being endlessly crushed beneath her own dreamed heel, made her burst into what she called kaleidoscopic tears—not because she had lost her glasses but because she had heard a sad story on the radio. Little children in nearly every part of the world were going about with no glasses at all, the radio announcer said, and you could send them your old pairs of lenses when you were through with them.

It was time to stop eating, she thought, when little children had so little to eat that they must give up seeing. And so it was, she thought, today three of us have lost our glasses, or perhaps even more—if you were to consider not only Exceedingly Thin Grandpère but also the poor little girl who might have received them and all to whom she might have handed them when she had finished her own observations of the world. Perhaps the would-be recipient of the glasses might have had a pair of dusty-footed twins for brothers who would surely have shared in combative attempts at enlightenment. Even Beatrice was not adolescent enough to wish to deny a pair of brothers a chance to see their whereabouts.

Who on earth could think of eating, she said to herself, having come up with at least two more reasons for the fast which had been going on now for ten whole days and was soon to be the tenth nocturnal. She knew now and was not afraid to say to herself, or to anyone who came to visit her: "This dwarf is in a darkened frame of mind."

ELEVEN

Floods, Droughts, Elvish Effluvium

One day Beatrice again looked up to find that the members of her immediate family were not listening to her thoughts on nomenclature, or on anything else. In the hazy light of the summer evening, seated around the big oak table before the open window, they had set to devouring corn muffins that were as golden as the fuzzy bottoms of bumblebees. These insects Beatrice had reveled in discovering in a boysenberry bush, when once as a tiny child she had lived briefly on Grandmère's old farm. Even though she had come up close to the bees, no harm had come to her. She had even managed to stroke one of the black hoops on its yellow back before it had flown off down the lane, past the row of wild roses that she understood to be still flourishing there. She had seen such bees painted onto the tin cans of honey that were brought to her by the owner of the local apiary. The dwarf remembered the time of the bee as the best period in her life—not long after which she had been confined to her basket, and after which she had never grown. For all I know, she thought out loud, the bees

I saw as a little child might have grown as large my own Grandmère by now. In response, Grandmère buzzed about the cradle, dancing and dusting her charge playfully with a dish towel.

Still, Beatrice could not help noticing that all the corn muffins had been devoured. No one at the table had even offered her a crumb to tempt her from her fate. The members of her family were speaking at that time rather nastily about the owner of the local egg factory she soon realized. This entrepreneur of eggs was named Adam Baum, and according to even Grandmère, he was purchasing all the farms in their region, one by one, for use as further sprockets in his expanding ring of poultry processing plants. Although this was not an unreasonable topic, an unusually acrid venom seemed to flow about the room that made Beatrice sit up and wring her hands on the edge of her basket and silently cry.

"Well, if we don't want to go buck naked and hungering, we'll have to sell something," Grandpère coughed into a clean handkerchief. "Pigs are gone." He was a tall and dignified man, Grandpère was. Substantial, Grandmère said.

"Corn is dead," Uncle Thibault burst in. "Rats et all the beans. And thet bank is worse than rats." Uncle Thibault, she had noticed, nicked his hairline daily on their doorframe as he came over from his little cottage out back. Uncle Thibault seemed to her merely an idiot.

"But, what's happened to the hamsters?" Beatrice asked,

propping herself up on the edge of her berth. Then an odd thing happened. Everyone, even both grandparents, turned to stare at her in complete astonishment. "Please, you can tell me," Beatrice inquired. "Did the hamster crop survive?'

Suddenly her whole family began to roar: her mother covered her face with her long thin hands in glee, peeking out at her father and covering her face again. It would seem that her question had nearly killed her brother Raulf, for there he was, nearly choking to death. His head was down between his knees and the edge of his chair, and the most hideous rasping had burst out of him. "Do something!" Beatrice cried as her brother nearly choked to death. With that admonishment, Loup knocked Raulf fully to the floor with a fierce blow to the upper back. Raulf did not bother to get up. "Hamsters!" Raulf choked. It seemed she had started a refrain. Again and again, they joined in to screech it and then when it had sputtered out, some one of them would venture even half the word. The uproar commenced again. To her it looked as if they had all drunk the same potion and taken on independent seizures about the room. As soon as they had stopped, all one of them had to do was point at her. Soon every last one was standing over her container and gesturing.

"Hamster!" they screamed.

"Well, you said the hamster crop was endangered, didn't you?" Beatrice asked.

"The 'hamster crop'!" they squealed. The Beautiful Mother had to sit back down. She beat her fist on the dictionary, repeating the would-be saint's words as though she had said something utterly delightful. The littlest lady could not help but smile while receiving such seemingly jovial attention for once; but she could not for the life of her see what it was all about, particularly during the dire discussion that had just been engrossing them. She had never seen her mother look so lovely as she did right then in the tempest of her giddiness. Even kind Grandpère sniggered against his will.

"Well, what is it?" she cried.

Finally, Raulf and Loup stared down at her, sputtering. "You're the hamster!" they shouted out in tandem, and then they were off again screaming and pounding one another on the back. The little lady lay back down again, stunned under her lace coverlet until she felt a tug at her sleeve. "They've always raised pigs and grain on this farm, my darling. I think it must have been a joke someone told you," Grandmère whispered in her ear. "That's the way it is, Sweetheart."

The breath swept out of her and she lay back down. Her family seemed to fade away. "Oh," she said in a voice that was tiny even for her. "Oh. I see."

Her father plunged down into his chair, his elbows on his knees. He was chewing on his fist and then he was involved in the earlier conversation as though it had never been halted by their farcical exchange. "We haven't got enough money to move back to the Territories—"

"And, it's too late for planting anything else," Immense Grandmère, her only ally, said. "Least wise, it won't do us any good, not soon enough."

"If we were in the Territories, we could start up the winter cabbages. That wouldn't be too late," Papa G. said.

"Stop all that talk about the Territories. It makes me pine," The Beautiful Mother moaned.

"I'm not going back to any Territories with anyone. You can't make me," Loop said.

"And I agree!" Raulf said.

"Shush," their mother said. "I have a last idea."

"What, Claudie?" Uncle Thibault whined, more lucidly. "This house amn't worth a thing."

"I'm not talking about selling the house, Thibault."

"What is it then?" Papa G. asked. The Beautiful Mother turned and slowly her sleeveless arm came up. With certain glee, she pointed toward Beatrice's face. "She's got hoards of people coming around to the house for her advice, hasn't she? She gives free advice, does she not? She won't even eat. She's got penniless notions of becoming some kind of sacrifice. We give her room and board. Well, don't stare at me like that. It's not as if your sister's done anything for any of us. She hasn't even taken the time to grow for goodness' sake. It's time we took charge. Take charge, and really charge for her, I say, from all those yokels on my new linoleum who want to hear her say, Be Good, Do Good. It's enough to make a beautiful person sick."

"That linoleum isn't new, Claudette—" Papa G. put in humbly enough.

"Tracks is tracks!" Uncle Thibault shouted getting into the mood.

"Charge?" Raulf scorned. "To listen to her? Who would come and pay to hear her yap? Free is one thing, paid is carp."

"Carp?" Loup taunted. "Carp? Haven't you got that turned around, Raulf?"

"I said 'carp,' and that is what I meant."

"Thank you, Raulf, for that one moment of civility." Grandmère said, heading toward the door with the water pail, "Your mother is just a bit hysterical, and for good reason. She doesn't really mean to sell our Bea, Raulfy."

"We'll see. We'll see," her mother said once Grandmère was well beyond the window and had passed the scorched petunia patch moving toward the pump. "I've got ideas, if that doesn't turn out to work."

"Ah, Mom, I amn't goin to work on no one else's farm," Loup whined out. "I already worked enough."

"There there, boys," their mother said. "Beatrice has got plenty of resources and great salesmanship as well. And if that doesn't save the farm from that egg sucking Adam

Baum, well—in May the circus always does come to this town—"

"Mother!" Beatrice cried out.

"Look on the bright side," her mother said. "You'd look a lot better in a pair of tights up on the high wire—or on an itty bitty dog on a barrel than lying about untouched in that basket with a bunch of local yokels kneeling at your feet."

"But, Mama," one of her twin brothers pointed out, "Bea can't walk."

"Then they can strap her on, can't they? A person has to learn somehow to do a few things in this life."

"What was that, Claudette, you said about the circus coming to town?" Grandmère called, bringing in the water pail and dropping in the dipper. "Why, I haven't seen a good circus around here in so long. What was that about a dog?"

"Oh nothing," her beautiful daughter called back as she went in to sit at her desk. She took up the newspaper and pulled the pencil out from behind her ear. "We were just talking entertainment. It seems these hot days, Mother, the Twins can find nothing at all to do to entertain themselves, unless it's making hamster jokes—That is always a good laugh!" She began to sputter then, but managed to stop herself by not looking anywhere near the cradle. All the men-folk, teenagers included, rushed out onto the porch, chortling and looking to have a relaxation smoke.

TWELFTH NIGHT

After the Advent of Ink

In her first eighteen years, it seemed, she had always planned to write down her philosophies, necessarily with a felt-tipped pen because then she could hold the paper on her dwarfed knees while lying on her assorted dwarfed pillows, and the ink always would be reliably flowing then even against the undeniable force of gravity. One of her new philosophies was that she was much older than she seemed. Much more time surely passed while lying inactive in a cradle than while traversing even a mundane earth. Yet, whenever she dreamed of writing about this passage of time, the time went very swiftly. For this one thing, she was truly grateful; she was also grateful, she told herself, to have been born somewhat after the advent of ink in case she might ever get around to using it at length.

On this day, she was thinking as always upon her family's increasing age and the fact that she intended to live well into the end of the twenty-first century, unless, of course, she happened to starve to death. This paradoxical plan she planned to address on the morrow or even the next day.

And then too there was the matter of how one particular gnomish activist began writing about the very beginning of all that she herself knew to be true. As for what she would activate in her life, she had no idea really. Whatever it was, Beatrice was certain, she would soon find out. Perhaps, she thought, the dwarf-greatest accomplishment would be to activate herself. Yes, she thought, she would think upon that after she had completed thinking about her first eighteen years.

An Unlucky Day

Perhaps it is easy to imagine that at least from a distance, the temporarily fasting miniature lady looked like an infant. Nevertheless, up close she looked quite adult. Beatrice believed herself to resemble yet another image. She thought that she must look very much like a newly dried, recently wrung-out wash rag, very pale to be sure, and somewhat clean, such was her so-called defaced self-esteem. Every year after she had seen her fifteenth year, Beatrice looked younger to her visitors almost as though she were reversing time in her crib. Now with her intentional loss of weight she grew more mature, the townspeople said; and they had been visiting her ever since the time when she had resigned herself at the age of two to the very same wood and wicker wrapped nest that bore her still.

Of this change in her appearance, Beatrice had heard whisperings from among her callers, all of whom came to her with serious collateral information about the world and their places in it. Since she readily admitted that nearly all geographical information was new to her, it made for a stimulating exchange. Being almost entirely self-taught, her knowledge was nearly impenetrable. For her part, Beatrice could offer solace and advice that stemmed from an unquestioned innocence, an impartial view. Never did an argument break out between her visitors and herself. Troubled, they arrived, their faces creased, often streaked as if with the tears of enormous prehistoric mythic beasts. Radiating an inner light and confidence, they departed for the comfort of their homes.

How it happened was also a mystery to the dwarf. A certain peacefulness passed between them; that was all that could be said, a few words were exchanged. When it was over, she fell into a deep and exhausted sleep. It was as if they had drained her blood out by way of her ankles. By mid-week she would begin to recover; by the afternoon before her weekly session, she had sprung back to life. With the memory of their joy, she felt further renewed.

The local villagers had told her that observing the members of her family—but for her kindly grandparents—was like staring at the backdrop of painted rubber plants at the natural history museum. Maybe it was on the whole interesting, they said, but it was not looking at the very animal that one had come to see—be it stuffed bear or raccoon.

Increasingly now, it grew difficult for Beatrice to slip off to sleep for all her newly troubled thoughts. As knowledge of the townspeople's resentments against her family, on her behalf, crept into her family's consciousness, their alienation began to grow, so much so that the thought was not inconceivable to Beatrice that her mother and brothers might actually sell her to the passing circus where, it was well known, even the prettiest of their painted ponies could barely hobble into the ring for lack of nutriments. Hearing of this, many a letter she had written to their ring master; but perhaps her brothers had failed to provide the requisite stamps. Each week on a Sunday afternoon, her two teenaged brothers, unbeknownst to her mother, had begun to entertain her visitors while they waited outside in line to speak with her. At such times, her brothers attempted to turn the villagers' hearts against her with tales of their own supposed subservience.

She first heard it through her window when a guest, who preferred to remain nameless, opened the shutters for her.

That day under her window, the Twins reported that her family's hatred for her had its genesis in certain supposedly irrefutable facts. First of all, it was unfair, the Twins whined—while reading from notes they had scribbled on wide-lined low-grade paper—that their sister received such devoted attentions when she never did a thing to help their mother around the house.

Already their complaints, so general in nature, seemed

dubious. The miniature lady could hear booing and stamping from the crowd outside her window. The boys stood their ground. She, the boys declared, a slougher and malingerer, was in actuality no saint at all, not even an aspiring one.

Trying beyond their capacity to make a point, they said, Beatrice was kind beyond all basis in reality, she was sickeningly kind, nothing but an idle flatterer. It made the brothers want to gag. Twin youthful gagging sounds accompanied this. She pictured them, red hair aflame, fingers aimed down gargoylish throats.

For example—the elder Twin said to her horror, gaining confidence in his slightly more nasal voice—she was always on some remote philosophical quest which by the nature of her stubborn immobility had somehow to involve them. Two innocent twins they were, barely out of adolescence, who had no time to themselves to develop any sort of private philosophy of their own. No time whatsoever, they declared. They were being denied time to do their homework and advance themselves. Why, they had nearly failed out of school; and each of them had had to repeat several grades.

Yes, they shouted, gathering steam. They were so busy caring for her—these traitors announced—that when they were not actually washing her things and trying to make her eat, they were washing her actual body. This untruth set her gasping into her pillows, so much so that the loyal guest, a member of European royalty, grew alarmed. After all Grandmère, as everyone knew, was the miniature lady's sole caretaker. The anonymous visitor placed a cloth on her forehead. Yes! Yes! the boys were heard to expound with increasingly imaginative glee. Everyday, every minute it seemed they were set to brushing her long and very tangled tresses. They must polish her nails—not just her hands but her tiny toes also. They might as well have been required to enroll in Alice Palmer's School of Enticing Beauty for all the time they spent icing her lips, oiling her feet and backside against the sores that came from lying about so long in a basket. And was that not enough to ask of two innocent boys who were trying to go to school by day and to work farm chores before and after school and also long into the evening? The crowd had begun to stamp their feet in agreement now.

When the Twins were not engaged in the difficulties of all these groomings the boys invented, then they were forced to spend their youthful hours singing chansons. Chansons, they argued, which she had pitifully tried to copy down from the educational radio. Chansons! When they might have been out representing their county in international football, if they had only had the chance to go out for it.

A little sob erupted from Raulf's voice; she would have known that false note anywhere. Many were the times it had gotten him an added scoop of iced strawberries or even out of school on mid-term examination days.

Forced into subservience by a miniature lady's harsh yet desperate voice, Raulf said, they had tried relentlessly to sing these chansons properly—without any classical training and in the face of the occasional errors she made in copying by ear—which, they said, made them look, so they thought, utterly ridiculous.

All their friends, especially the girls, laughed at them from the hillock behind their house while they were forced to sing—and that was not all of it. The songs had been followed by yet other dwarf-care-taking chores.

She heard a certain grumbling in the populace outside and a sound like fingernails scratching along the casement of the door. She imagined a scene as out of Frankenstein, complete with rakes and hoes, splintering window glass. How long might she have to live before she met an untimely sibling-generated death? The fasting lady could not be sure.

FOURTEEN

A True Friend

The following day the baker's wife had to wrap Beatrice in her own beautiful, yeast-scented shawl and carry her about the room until she simmered down. "Hold me to the window, hold me to the window!" Beatrice demanded. "I will tell them the truth! How can they listen to such oddities?"

"Calmer, calmer!" the baker's wife encouraged. "Have a little dignity. Besides, they've long ago decided to go home. What will your grandmother say when she comes back from town?"

It was true, she told the baker's wife, that the boys never could copy music properly, much less sing it; that's why she had not encouraged them past the initial ten minute attempt. And never once did the Twins call her sister in their oration, except in the religious sense. Those insensitive, twin, buck-teethed brutes, she lamented.

But on the third day, when the baker's wife was kind enough to come before dawn, after the braided oatmeal breads and babka had been put out in the glass cases, the crowd assembled again to hear the boys continuing: These chores, they declared, publicly, right outside her door, to all her celebrants who were waiting, just then, for hours on end, just to have a word with her—

She was much too exhausted, Beatrice claimed, to be lifted out of bed. She could see the backs of the Twins' red heads as the baker's wife held up the make-believe mirror along with providing her own mature account as witness to the crime. Between the vision she had imagined and the account of the mesmerized baker woman, Beatrice knew that her twin brothers had overturned the hay wagon and were standing on top of it not more than thirteen feet from her window. "But why didn't Raulf and Loup just get into the hay wagon?" she asked, taken aback by this foolishness. "Now Papa G. and Exceedingly Thin Grandpère will have to turn it over and load it up again." The bakery woman didn't need to say a thing. In the relative universe of their village, the twin nature of her brothers was somewhat universally understood.

"These concocted chores, concocted by a dwarf with no destination or occupation or benefit to society, have to be fulfilled by ourselves," her brothers proclaimed, "by ourselves who have yet to even go to college, or even to think about going to college, or even to drink at any bar in the county—legally, that is."

Triumphantly and entirely erroneously, they listed her

daily requirements of them, to a suddenly solemn crowd: The Twins were responsible, they said, for all of the following (Horrific lies! Beatrice screamed into the Baker Woman's collarbone):

✠ *Selecting special purple fruits of unknown and, for all they knew, illegal origin from the market to squeeze into the soup pan they were forced to bathe her in,*

✠ *Stripping and dunking her in said hot bath waters,*

✠ *Hunting red-faced in girly shops for Little Lindy and Glamorous Gloria clothes that wouldn't make her look fat or bulbous even in a crib,*

✠ *Looking for bows for her very small waist which she always liked to emphasize,*

✠ *Making endless appointments for all her callers who came to ask advice or read religious passages to her,*

(She could hear the crowd mumbling now: "She never once gave an appointment to me." "Did you have an appointment?" "No, I never did even get offered one!")

✠ *Rearranging appointments for her hundreds, now thousands of visitors,*

❧ *Calling back to list after list of clients to confirm their arrival times,*

❧ *Wiping her nose when she was sick so she wouldn't spoil her newly polished nails on the lace handkerchiefs they were forced to embroider her absurd initials onto by candlelight so as not to disturb her sleep with the grating sound of needles pricking cloth.*

("Her initials are M.D.," one of the ladies shouted outside their house. "That is the truest thing I've heard all day. Get those poor mad boys out of my way, I'm going in! I've got to get to work!")

"There now, calm thyself," the womanly baker said, wiping the miniature lady's nose and starting to blubber as if on cue. "I know, I know, your own brothers! I never had a brother. It's just too cruel!"

❧ *"And cooling her brow," the boys went on, enumerating as if infinitely. She could see their new freckles popping out under the rising heat of the sun.*

❧ *Cooling her brow with hand-knitted (by ourselves, no less) tiny damp cloths because that obsequious dwarf is constantly afflicted with contagious fevers in wintertime."*

✤ *And doing healing favors, such as holding her down so that we might pour her favorite cough medicine—it smells like tar—down her throat. She likes the effect,* Loup said, *but hates the flavor. Since she could never give a clear message about her own requests,* Raulf complained, *they were left feeling incessantly guilty even after such hard work.*

✤ *And even worse,* Loup sighed rather convincingly, *there is the cleaning out of her ears and nostrils with tiny cotton swabs.*

Beatrice stifled a cry.

✤ *And the restringing of her mystical beads,* Raulf said.

✤ *After she has a fit,* Loup put in.

Through the crack in the door opening, friends and penitents began to spy at her; in turn, she could see the twins on top of the hay cart, bobbing their red heads in unison and swallowing hard upon their freckled lies. Their Adam's apples jugged up and down. At the sight of her staring over the edge of her basket at them, those next in line looked at their feet long enough to begin the excuse of kicking the mud-rail beside the door.

Waiting to speak with her, the neighbors listened on as her brothers spelled out, even further, why it was not she who should be declared a saint but they—the first Twin Saints, to their knowledge, in the county's history.

It was a tribute—she would say later to Grandmère—to their local countrymen that they could bear up for such a long period of time in line while assailed by such dolts as God ever gave a sister, this pair of brothers assigned to her on the same fatefully rotten day and hour.

The Twins actually cried now, sniffling and mewling disgustingly. They had moved onto the invention of even more demanding tasks. In other circumstances, she would have been proud of their whimsy. Considering their lack of intellectual endowment, even these speeches were considered locally to be miracles bestowed upon them by the presence of their sister, the reigning dwarf. The Twins went on to recite the deeds they were supposedly forced by her to do, their heartless and increasingly gigantic-seeming taskmaster.

The Little Wonder, they said, forced them into so very much:

※ *The bearing of alms, for instance,*

※ *And, the patching up of all used household clothing. Her clothing, the boys declared, was completely and hopelessly rent into frazzles during her frenzies, which they themselves were forced to reconstruct,*

※ *The carrying of goods to even poorer persons than themselves after the locating of even poorer persons than the previously poorer persons than themselves entailing the heinous embarrassment of bestowing these gifts as gifts from a dwarf and not even from themselves—*

The boys had begun to ramble a bit hysterically, yet they held up well considering their age.

❧ *They had received absolutely no credit whatsoever for their time spent darning and mending under a poor light with hair-thin needles because she claimed she could not tolerate bright light even when she was trying to read.*

❧ *There was much more, so much more, they declared. They muttered it publicly and between themselves, while now collecting moneys, under the instruction of their mother, from the increasingly poor people outside the door, whom she insisted she should see for free.*

Yes, yes! they said again and again, right there within her earshot. So it was said by her own kin:

❧ *The carrying of her willow leaves with which at night she liked to beat herself—gently but firmly, they swore, until small red welts in the shapes of rose buds climbed up on her back before the fireplace. No, no, she never once beat them.*

❧ *The fire must be kept fully lit and unobscured by chairs, or even their muddy boots after planting and harvesting, out of the line of her vision from her cradle. They went on more and more feebly in substance and more and more loudly in presentation, their voices squeaking like chains in their rusted swing set of yore.*

✠ *And the upkeep of a dwarf was a great expense for their dear mother, who flagged, even in her great beauty, under the weight of it in fiscal, physical, and mental vigor.*

✠ *Beatrice was so demanding, they said. Yes, they said, if it weren't for this self-centered resident dwarf, they themselves might have hired out to work on a neighbor's farm with all the other boys during the haying season as well as for spring planting and then detasseling in addition to working on their own farm. The financial foundation of the family, if it weren't for her, might have been secure.*

Was there no stopping the monsters? This, the baker woman and Beatrice asked one another. None too soon, they were joined by the baker. As it was, the robust cakebakers bound the Tiny One's arms with theirs and held her back so that she would not fling herself like a flying squirrel out the window upon her vociferous brothers.

As it was, the boys were announcing, their family stood to lose the farm to the notorious egg farmer Adam Baum, and then where would this Dwarf Star be, wandering about and homeless, The Miracle Dwarf, her brothers challenged, holding out pitiful collection vessels by their hat brims.

The Twins did not leave it at that; by sundown their story had grown, as had the offerings. Nonetheless, her callers, one after another, came in to see her, a little less wealthy after twin intimidations and their emotive shakedown. The baker woman declined to leave her side, even when her husband left to man the bread shop. One after another, the miniature lady's callers sat; and, for the first time, it was they who listened, and then out they went shaking their heads. Together with the baker woman, several citizens helped to wrap a slab of rising dough around the dwarf's forehead as a poultice. They massaged her feet to stop her incessant attempts at a non-stop self-defensive discourse.

Yes, soon throughout the village it was heard that the Twin Brothers of the Child of Innocence, both reckless teenagers—of an age she herself had been not so many months before—had made the final and least forgivable in their list of allegations: Supposedly, Beatrice had made the young and impressionable boys responsible, against their will, for bearing her favorite flowered thorns to the holy statue at the Crossroads near the old cemetery.

⁜ *In this same rite, she had made them equally answerable, they declared, for a weeping pious return on hands and knees along the newly graveled Purgatory Road. And who, but for a dwarf who would not even try to walk, could avoid knowing what sharp stones littered the road up from the beach past the new quarry toward Abington?*

⁂ *And when they were supposed to be doing their homework, they were forced by The Midgie, as they occasionally found the opportunity to call her, they were forced to read from long ancient philosophical passages, which they could not understand, aloud, to the lazy creature in the basket—*

⁂ *She, who only claimed to be their sister (after all, where was the resemblance?), indeed claimed all their time and indecent amounts of their attention.*

⁂ *This dwarf, they repeated yet again in their impassioned statements, who had been cast by an ill fate upon their innocent family, had refused to be carried out of the house even once in the past fifteen years,*

⁂ *This dwarf, who could extract guilt from the stone Civil War Monument in front of the town library, held her tiny iron fist over them. No matter that it was hardly bigger than a pencil eraser. It was a curse, they said, how relentlessly she had never once raised her voice nor complained in any human way about the insensitivity of Mother Nature in giving her a truncated stature or even in meting out a predictable weather scenario—even when the weather was sweltering in the house and every one of them, particularly the Twins, wished to be together with their teenaged friends at Bullrider's Creek—buff-naked and screaming and jumping off cliffs into the soothing coolness of water.*

If she had not known it all to be untrue, she might have wept herself for them, the poor unfortunate brothers of an exquisitely shaped and talented, if tiny, person.

Never so clearly was it repeated to her as when her cousin, Christopher, a true saint, dropped in on her. But that would not be for some time yet, at least twelve hours. And twelve hours was not an insignificant amount of time when one was fasting with determination toward ultimate sainthood.

During this time Beatrice became so upset that she had to have her teeth pried from the corner of a half-chewed day-old biscuit some penitent had thoughtlessly left beside her basket. She was thinking in rhymes now, but she noticed they were all nouns sounding oh so similar. All verbs had dropped out of her life. Slowly it became obvious that there was little motion in the room even when it came to air currents. The loyal baker and his wife took turns until it was time to bake the morning cinnamon bread. Yes, they tried their hands at animated readings and then at fanning the comic section near her face until they wore her out and she drifted into a fitful lack of consciousness.

FIFTEEN

True Saints

When the one called the Cousin, also called Christopher, also known as A Real Saint, finally arrived bearing a mirror as a gift, he found Beatrice particularly responsive, much to his surprise. He had pictured her quite otherwise. He held up the walnut hand mirror he had carved and silvered for this his first homage to his second cousin on his father's side, the dwarf. On the fifteenth day of her renowned fast, he too noticed that her face, like her voice, was very soft and full, and around her head grew a spiky radiance. As she gazed for the first time into his mirror, she was so startled by her own appearance that she hardly noticed Cousin Christopher.

"Cousin," she said to him, "it is the first time in my life that I have clearly seen my face. My family had thought it most kind to keep the secret from me. Tell me, Cousin. Do you find me pathetic? Or are you here, like the others, for good luck?" This she asked calmly on the advice of the baker woman, perhaps even with a hint of boredom. It was good luck to touch a dwarf on the forehead, every visiting penitent knew that, and everyone did it when they came to call on her. Often at the end of the day she would have a sore spot, dead center on her forehead, where the masses had rubbed raw a tender portion.

But Cousin Christopher restrained himself. Or perhaps the one called the Cousin already knew that he was his own good luck; he did not need to take luck from dwarves, or from anyone, through his fingertips. Already a certain rapport began.

"Oh then," he said, as on she stared into the silvered looking glass. "I thought since it was my first sight of you, Cousin Beatrice, that we might share the same experience." Together they gazed into the reflector. "It is better to share such things as often as possible."

The Cousin also pointed out on his first and quite congenial visit that her use of the words "my family" while portraying the hostile feelings of one or even three members of a family, when there were six or seven of them living on the property, was inaccurate and self-defeating. Did she not have a dog for a companion? No, he had heard that Rude Raoul had been carried away into the next county by hawks. If she had had a dog still, she would not have been so dejected.

In response to his tabulations about her family, she sighed, making her point. And then she said that she found it very difficult to count those who acquiesced as on one's own side, particularly if their silence was used in active support of one's nemesis.

"Nemeses," the Cousin corrected, as rapidly they gained rapport. "It is hardly right to reduce one's enemies to one only, when there are actually three."

"And a few scabs," she interjected jauntily.

"Precisely," the very tall cousin said. "That would be silly, perhaps even remotely dangerous."

Overcoming for the first time an innate shyness he had always been troubled with, the Cousin then conjectured aloud: There was bound to be resentment in something called by everyone on this continent, and perhaps even abroad, 'The Dwarf Family,' "when every last one of them but you is well over six feet tall."

"I know, I know," she sighed paradoxically. "What they have to endure on my account!" And, her smile sparkled, "Exactly how tall are you?"

"Let's not talk about it," the Cousin said. "I'm a little sensitive about my height."

She raised her head up off the pillow to peer over the side of the basket. "I thought you were," she said. "You know, I just thought perhaps you were. And I'll bet you're still growing?"

"Unfortunately, I am," the Cousin said, slouching further down in the straight-backed chair. She admired the crispness of the points in his white collar.

"What is it?" she said. "You simply have to tell me—six feet eight?"

"Nine," he said, dropping the elegant fringe of his charcoal lashes.

"And growing?" Her little hands flew up to her cheeks like baby starfish.

"I have pains in my hips and shins."

"I'll bet you do!" she cried. "I'll bet you have them pretty fierce. I ache from head to toe sometimes from lack of growing. My mother—who is very beautiful—tells me it's because I refuse to move. I don't know." She tugged her blanket up around one shoulder and peered out over it.

"I suspect it's the other way around, Miss Bea. When I ache, I hate to move a thing."

"Really and truly?" she called out, wagging her tousled head again over the basket's side. "You're not just saying that?" But she could see it in his expressive eyes, his complete sincerity—in everything. "Thank you very much," she said, "from the bottom of my heart."

"In any case," the Cousin declared—looking into her azure eyes a long time, then clearing his throat repeatedly—he would call again. He shifted his long limbs, nearly knocking over the bedside lamp. He found her lovely, "in a spiritual way," he said. "And, otherwise."

"Would you like to touch my forehead?" she asked, "for luck? It might take away your pain."

"No!" the Cousin gruffly stated. But he would return tomorrow with a bit of fruit. He would not demand that she eat it, but merely that she look at it, he said.

When he lowered his head and shoulders so that he might pass out of her vision, and then in a flash had lurched out the door and down the rosy lane, she lay back and wept. He, the only one she had truly wanted to give it to, would not take her magic touch.

II

This is the way it is remembered in a certain Book of Dreams, how seventeen years before a certain self-imposed fasting, and only two years after the first real adventure of her birth, she and The Beautiful Mother had set out on another:

Away on a train, first out of the city sounds, out of the automobile city, wheeling across countryside that flattened and opened and then finally after a day and a night of rocking that way in The Beautiful Mother's arms, up against the full breasts, cradled against the maternal belly—which only later would she come to understand contained her twin sacrosanct brothers—away on their adventure, a premature walker went with her Beautiful Mother.

Sun infiltrated the carriage of the train, glazed the dwarfish face and hands, while Beatrice, a late nurser, clung, thrilled as a hummingbird, to the then kind Beautiful Mother's swollen upper torso. The tip of one breast, hard as a small rubber hose, piped a natural nourishment, ceaselessly flowing, between her gums. With the rhythm of the train, the two would-be siblings in her mother's belly continued their filial hum. A sense of well being, the baby Bea thought, encompassed them all; yet under the soles of her baby slippers, a significant battle had begun. As far as Beatrice could tell from the ruckus, The Beautiful Mother had eaten live fishes. Or squirrels perhaps. Certainly something unlucky had found its way deep down inside.

In the aisle, the man in the leaf-green hat stood up and sat down, calling out periodically odd names, even the names of pyrogenic rocks, foreign places and animals, it seemed, and magically starting and stopping the train with each utterance, a tug on his little cord, and a flip of his ticket book. "Gridlock! Blue Ridge! Rock Ridge! Amethyst! Roseville-Benton!"

The smallish child leapt on the seat into the light from the window and then into the lamplight and again onto the naked breasts—until finally The Beautiful Mother detached herself, buttoned both their jackets, and lurched into the aisle of the yet catapulting car, thrusting Beatrice into her pocket book, feet first into the open seam.

Already the little child screamed.

A low dirge simultaneously arose from the rail cars, along with a loud hubbub under the tram, and then the final screech of metal hurting metal. The Beautiful, Very Gravid Mother conveyed young Beatrice up the aisle under one arm. Surely The Beautiful Mother would have fallen on this her own daughter if the man in blue had not caught them during her brief but potentially deadly misstep. Onto the platform, a second old gentleman safely handed them down.

"Carefully now, Youngish Lady! You mighta unstrung all your younguns, inside and out, those mites sprung and unsprung. Mighta blightened your gorgeous body, which is a pleasure from God clearly seen. Some lucky soul has already begotten it, it is plain! All the more sorrowful, I surely am! Step right out'n the traffic before you all are run down and lookin' like squash under the feet—I remember one time, an elderly gent—" The old man's white brush mustache quavered on tirelessly.

The Beautiful Mother, exquisite, auburn-haired, most radiant, with a pearly complexion blushed up sensually at the cheeks, transmitted her admittedly short legs across the platform, bearing, with as much dignity as possible, considerable extra weight on her nearly normal frame. The Beautiful Mother stared out into the arena of family fields.

Beatrice clambered upwards and slantwise out of the satchel over the hummock of her mother's white cotton jacket, gripping tightly to the brittle lace collar of the satin blouse beneath—to see what it was that had hypnotized her mother so. The tot craned her own eyes and neck. "Mama," she said, "Mama, Mama!" They were in the biggest room Beatrice had ever seen.

Above them: from horizon to horizon, a glass dome hovered, blue without error. And all else was flat and endless, decidedly verdant, clear over there to the two toy trees that worked steadily, Mama said, to dust the rim of a plate-like earth.

Beside the red brickyard on which they stood, the train station squatted, also brick. And there before them, two roads swept oddly away, curving through jet-black dirt and newly germinating corn, so her mother pointed out. Then The Beautiful Mother began pulling Beatrice inexplicably away from the warmth of the maternal neck. Immense, alien arms brushed against the child then, and it was done. The Beautiful Mother had thrust Beatrice into a strange woman's grasp. The Beautiful Mother said something most peculiar indeed: "Thank you, Mama," she said.

Beatrice, as she remembered it, had only seen one Mama in this landscape and her Mama had just handed her off to a woman drawn as full and round in the scene as an immense cage ball. Out the top and bottom of her torso, her long elegant limbs and neck stuck out. What a striking yet unknown face!

"Shush," The Beautiful Mother said. "It's hard enough. Shush now."

"Falling! Falling!" the wee-some child screamed.

"Shush!" The Beautiful Mother said.

"Wait right there," someone shouted.

"Falling!" the child screamed, convinced they had fallen into the center of some experimental jar.

Already she was crying it out as her mama patted the tiny tresses and turned her back. Farther and farther away, cutting the courtyard into triangles, steering the portentous womb past the locomotive, The Beautiful Mother went. The long straight hair of her little mother bobbed at the back of her knees. Then up the steps her mother veered with the assistance of two smiling porters, until—alas—The Beautiful Mother had disappeared once again entirely into the train.

All this while Beatrice called out the only name she knew her by, again and again, screaming it after her Mama, as the train pulled away and the one called Grandmère pumped Bea's own little arm up and down in the socket, as the black metal object with the mama in it shot away. Up and down Beatrice's arm went as the large woman cried it out, "Say Bye, say Bye," over and over again.

Already a small crowd had begun to gather close by.

"Isn't she cute," someone said. "Isn't she cute now."

"She's so tiny, and look at those curls."

"What a little doll," someone asked. "Excuse me, is she your ordinary dwarf?"

"Look at those elfish sapphire eyes."

Grandmère's ponderous chest puffed out under Beatrice,

"There are no dwarves in this family!" Grandmère roared. "Come now, precious," she said to the baby dwarf in an entirely different voice. "Your Grandpère is waiting for you in his auto round back of this joint."

But Beatrice was calling it out. Her name. When she thought back on it in recurring fevers of hunger and weakness, she imagined her eyes to have been very big that day, big as the landscape, big as fear and all her imaginings of where The Beautiful Mother had gone. And then the new thought: whatever could she have done that was so terribly wrong, that could have made her own mama leave her behind, perhaps forever, in this land where sky was bigger than night terror and high buildings, where sky was everything: sky, that place—she already knew—where angels and dead people lived.

And they were mere dots on the open black-and-green speckled spring plain. So it seemed still, on the day numbered sixteen.

DAY SEVENTEEN

Substantial Comforting

Very early in the morning, even before the apricot light broke over the black dirt of the plains, Beatrice would wake, as still she did. Even as a baby she tuned herself to the first rising of birds. At their glorious beaked alarm, exclaiming along with their blazing dawn chorus, she would fly into her grandparents' room. "Shush, shush," Grandmère whispered—rather loudly, she later realized. "Grandpère is snoozing."

Up the stack of magazines and newspaper clippings she an early climber scrambled, clinging to the edge of the bedspread, hoisting herself into Grandmère's hands.

"Grandmère—" Bea whispered. "Grandmère," she said, curling herself completely under her grandmother's arms. Beatrice was to be the most petite of all the women in the family for all of time remembered.

"Yes, darling," Grandmère whispered back.

"I'll be quiet," Bea said.

"Yes, darling," Grandmère murmured. "Sleep now for awhile. The birds are playing accompaniment to your

Grandpère's good-morning song."

Up went the rattle of his snore, first faked, then turning toward real. His whistle fell away entirely when he was under the true spell of his dreams. While he slept, Grandmère petted the beloved dwarf, and she in turn patted her grandmother's heavy arms. Grandmère held each arm up and the sacks of her flesh fell down in two smooth folds, one under each bone, and overlapped to make two thick sweet-smelling quilts for the tiniest grandchild. Grandmère's forefinger came up then in front of her splendid smiling bow-like mouth. The child lay sighing against the soft pillow her grandmother's bosom made for her. "Shhhhh—" Grandmère said. Her finger made its tracings around and around the armholes of the baby's undershirt, lightly as a feather might, around and around, never ceasing, not for anything in the world, Grandmère said, being careful never to hold her uncomfortably too close.

EIGHTEEN

Another Early Kidnapping

Grandmère had been trying to bring the young adult dwarf out of her doldrums; yet, now Beatrice slept an alarming and deepening sleep. Grandmère had attempted, unsuccessfully, to offer nourishment by way of ripe orange slices pressed against the dozing dwarf's gums. But in the dwarf's ongoing reveries of infant bliss, Grandmère was cuddling her and placing her on top of the blaring old radio where she might try to dance. Finally Grandmère carried her out under the twisted apple tree and set the infant Beatrice gently beside her in the vast front seat of her immense automobile and whirled her five miles up the road to the house of Aunt Burnoose, although Beatrice was her name.

As the years passed, Aunt Burnoose insisted on recounting at each family gathering one Lilliputian child's very bad behavior when the relatives flocked in to stand beside her cradle for the holiday homage: "To think you got that far from us! And without anyone noticing. On those new butterfat legs! Why! I glanced up from hanging out my Monday laundry," Aunt Burnoose exclaimed, "and there you were, Beatrice, in those little yellow shorts: nothing but a bee on the horizon trundling away for Grandmère's house. How on earth did you know where to go? Thank god a tractor-trailer truck did not up and run you down! And you, soon after to be a dwarf that would never walk again! I have never seen anything like it! Have you? Have you? A dwarf child to walk nearly six miles and never walk again? Why! But then, have you ever seen another dwarf? Why? I guess I never have seen another dwarf either! When I think of it, I know a miracle has occurred in my life, saving a saint and a dwarf at the same time. A saint in the making. Doesn't take considerable to make a saint in this family. Call us dwarves if you like, there is only one dwarf here. I am glad to say it! And she is a saint. Pah! So there!"

Out away from the aunt's high freckled laughter, away from Beatrice's cousins' tall run-and-bully games. How did Beatrice know which way to run from Aunt Burnoose's cottage, toward Grandmère's house? Down the rutted dirt roads that ran like rivulets through the massive plantings of corn and beans, then onto the main gravel that stretched five point six miles through a sea of green to Grandmère's lane, right there toward Grandmère's Parisian scent and toward the small cherry-colored lips set like tiny fallen candles into her wrinkleless, creamy flowing, scented skin. The Immense Grandmère carried a fragrance that resembled powdered silk and rose beams if roses could beam, so the little baby thought. The dwarf runaway trundled now, quite of her own accord, toward the massive replacement for The Beautiful Mother who was yet far off and surely growing ghostly without her. In terrible trouble, The Beautiful Mother must be, this baby believed. Without her own little girl she was—somewhere.

The land rose and fell in gentle waves, cresting again and then again in the midst of broad open sky. The new corn unfurled its leaves: in stark straight rows like millions of khaki soldiers progressing—not much higher than the child herself. In gigantic formation, immense high-voltage towers spiked the boundless field.

Yet the only vision the little girl had in her head was her grandparents' white porch and barn. "The big house," Beatrice's cousins called it, they who all had the fortune to grow to more or less their share of normal size. "We all want to live in the big house! And we always will!"

Collectively the Cousins lived in a wilderness of distances, mere points on a chart among innumerable vectors. Or so they behaved. Too much movement in the world, they believed, might lead any one of them astray. All four children, the uncle and aunt, too, lived year-round in the romantic two-room peeling yellow cottage that had only recently been a chicken coop. Morning glories grew up and over the entirety of the outhouse out back—this their only facility, aside from the well and the one-bucket shower built into the back entryway. There any one of them might be accidentally happened upon, stripped down and hooting under a cold-water douse, upholding the family tradition of keeping clean. As has been said, this family never had any want for cleanliness. No sooner dirty, no sooner cleaned, they said. Their skin gleamed.

From the Cousins' house, only one set of buildings could be seen sprouting from the land and that was the barn, the shed, the garden house belonging to the 'big house.' There Grandmère and Grandpère lived in an elegance that was undeniable and relative. Between these two landmarks now, the peeling tiny yellow one and the white, along the graveled road, Beatrice a child of nearly three years took inventory, one foot on, then off, the grassy shoulder as an occasional car churned past, stirring smoke then dust and a jet stream of tiniest stones from behind each corrugated tire.

Two deep ditches had been dug in the plain, one on either side of the road, and in them grew wild roses gone thick with soft pink petals and attendant thorns. While releasing a friendly bumblebee, before she could realize what was happening, she had fallen into the ditch and pierced the centers of both palms. From this accident, she would recover rapidly with only two white scars like lozenges in her skin; but for now she held her hands up before her as she walked with only a small amount of blood trickling down. Even these injuries were not foremost in the toddler's mind. The road opened perpetually ahead of her, as though she were walking on a thread that bore the promise of her return to her own past and the face of her own, perhaps-dead, Beautiful Mother, and then—if not her own Mama—perhaps her square-jawed, cajoling Daddy miraculously beside the crib he had made for her in the Distant Territories, the two of them holding up, between them, her fiercely yapping little black lab. Or if not, then Grandmère might be there at the end, fat and tall as the one-story yellow house she had just fled. And there, too, the lanky, squeaking Grandpère, ever a source of cheer and good books.

But up behind her roared another sound. The beaten blue automobile pulled around as it ground to a finish, spitting gravel over its silver fins. Exhaust gadgets hung just in front of her, coiled, snake-like onto the road. Then a fierce hand, faster than a pop-gun, shot out and yanked her inside, there to sit bolt upright on the big front seat. Aunt Burnoose rotated the car in the road again, nearly careening into one ditch, and then another, before starting off.

Beatrice popped up in anxiety herself, pivoting before the dashboard, her eyes fixed backward on the shrinking white rectangular house. The hand pump next to her grandparent's house receded into a vision of nothing but a permanently flexed twig in the green lawn, a stone's throw from where the gnarled tree would, soon enough, be offering up its blushing apples. Beatrice cupped her injured palms together and did not say a word. The barn had already departed and then the roseate lane.

Now in the silver-blue interior of the seasoned automobile, all the screaming cousins had a hand on her, each one of them for luck, all the little parrots, reiterating what the mad driver in front, Aunt Burnoose, screeched again and again:

"No! No! No! Beatrice! Never! Never run away! No no!"

Slowly Beatrice became aware of it: a caring hand was on her arm. "Eat, honey-darling, you must eat," that same lost grandmother was insisting now, though nearly seventeen years beyond the memory. An effervescent sound superceded the usual barnyard background noise as she came slowly out of her reveries. By this time her belly was so shrunken that she did not even have her usual hunger pains. Her ears pricked up on the sides of her head. No, she could not discern whether it was the pump out back that she heard. Or was it? Beyond the sound of the rooster's morning reveille, her darling grandmother expressed hopelessness at the dwarf's hideous self-imposed frailties? "Why ever, my darling, won't you eat?"

Yet Beatrice now imagined herself inside another house

instead—the first one, the safe house, in the brownstone city from which The Beautiful Mother and she had set out one day, the one with the piano in the front room and the brown flowered rug. And there, too, the spindled chair in motion and in it a chestnut-haired Mama, with azure eyes like her own, rocking and singing while she, the solitary Beatrice, listened and tried to sing along.

Now there was no waking her for days, and it was in a fragmented past she lived:

"Stop sniffling," Aunt Burnoose was snapping. "Think! Here we all are together! Be glad! When, not three minutes ago, you were no more than a flea lost on the balls of a dog."

"Little flea bite!" the children joined in. "Our own weird mosquito," they entreated her: "Be glad. Be glad."

Beatrice threw her hurt baby hands onto her dwarf ears to stop their sounds. "Not a 'squito!" she sobbed. "Not a midgie. Not a midgie. Want to go home. Mama! Mama! Grandmère!"

"Ha!" Aunt Burnoose shouted good-naturedly, steering up her own lane. "You are at home, for today at least. Good God, is that blood coming out of your hands? Or is it coming out your ears? Stop howling and let me see! Oh, for heaven's sake!"

NINETEEN

One Family Reunited

In such country, come late summer, there is a sound rising from the very roots. By day, it whirls up the long drying stalks of corn, a pinwheel vibrating sound of dead leaves beating unhindered against the scorching atmosphere. By night, the whine of crickets so permeates the darkened countryside, so fills up all space beneath the broad deep and dazzling sky, that the sound itself is like a kind of light for the ears.

Come August in the same year of her abandonment to the country, a country which she would come eventually to love, Beatrice's mother—whom Bea had long now presumed to be dead and flying dejectedly overhead—reappeared, borne by the resounding metal wheels of a locomotive and all its dark traveling cars. Once again Bea watched from the platform for she didn't know what, while encompassed in the folds of Grandmère's arms. Then Beatrice was set, a mere butterfly, on her grandmother's huge hip.

Across the red brick platform, out of a crowd of rejoicing and crying greeters and the miraculously returned came—

miracle of miracles!—The Beautiful Mother, not much bigger than a child herself, between two porters carrying on their backs identical grotesquely scarred black trunks. Then, as if out of the Book of Dreams, there strode her own lanky father. And just behind them trotted—Beatrice had never thought to see him again!—her mangy little dog, Rude Raoul, barking at her daddy's heels.

Beside the tracks, the one named Uncle Thibault also stood, in his especially clean overalls and white turtleneck, kneading the rim of his own rarely worn grey felt hat. The skin had been scratched raw around his lower jaw in his attempt at quick shaving, his golden mustache cropped stiff as a currying brush, beneath his heavily-veined once-handsome nose. Fine red seams had begun more and more each day to saunter out toward the sides of his face, rising in bluish tints at the crests of each cheekbone. And his eyes, they too must once have been even lovelier, so clear they were and vacant a blue. The Beautiful Mother leaned up to kiss her brother's cheek. Aunt Bern had said it, within earshot of Beatrice more than once: "And you can't stop me saying it, I will say it again: Uncle Thibault lives a life of self-inflicted shock in that shed out there, back of Grandmère's house. That he does, that he does, your Uncle Thibault does. Keep your distance. More's the pity. Keep away. My brother-in-law is most insane!"

Beatrice had only seen Uncle Thibault standing up

once during the past ten months, while she had been living not fifty feet from his shack with her grandparents. Having hazarded a climb over the thorny trellis nailed to his makeshift hut, through his open window Beatrice had investigated. A ghoul in bed, he lay with a book across his face, his long bony hands intertwined and twiddling at his chest, whether asleep or not.

Now why does this frighten me?—she asked herself—when she herself had lain like this many times while resting in her crib, her eyes shaded completely, a fairy tale in her head, and the smell of ink and coloring books to ease her into a likely Book of Dreams.

It must have been Uncle Thibault's skin, she thought, the pallor and the way it clung to his bones like something viscous from atop some left-over Saturday soup on Wednesday. He was surely a little clammy, she thought while peering around the vines to which she clung.

In Beatrice's imagination, the trellis might very well have shaken or even collapsed whenever she took another look at him. To her, Uncle Thibault was the only unusual thing in the landscape—or so she thought. A chase might very well have ensued, she imagined, with Beatrice the one in sight, and mad Thibault quick after the little dwarf's heels. Yes, she had thought about that; but while recovering from thorny scratches, she had to admit that no such nightmare had so far occurred.

Only at night when Immense Grandmère and the rest of the family had gone to bed would Uncle Thibault find his way into the kitchen there to lean over the edge of the basket to leer. At first, it seemed to begin in dreams, and then too soon she knew well enough that it was real: the tremendous hands like aeroplanes landing on her nightgown in the midst of a sweet cloud of dreams, as Beatrice would wake to the odor that emanated from his prematurely rotting gums.

But, throughout the first portion of her childhood, Uncle Thibault merely slept, the one long oily candle flickering at the side of his bed table, his shirt stuck to his ribs with sweat, his grey pants like a stained, forked road atop his unmade bed. His belt lay loosely buckled around his bony hips, and the hole in his sock made one small and tidy necklace around the greying mushroom of his right big toe. Up, his chest puffed; then down it fumed, gently, occasionally with a sigh.

Yes, he was asleep or she would have leapt away from the vine like a flying squirrel and found herself so quickly at Grandmère's hem. And on he slept, making only two motions recognizable to her. First, his right hand came up beneath the book still lying over his face, in a dreamy way, and then his one finger went in under the corner, and swept something away.

It must, of course, have been a crocodile tear, because, quickly after, the same hand made the rapid sign of the cross from the Adam's apple that protruded from under the book to breastbone and then shoulder to shoulder. It was this sign then that sent her on the dwarf way. As all children, even small ones, know, these were not gestures made by anyone fast asleep—

Now again on the train platform, tight as a girdle, Grandmère's fat arms held her against the comfort of her ribs, away from mad Uncle Thibault and away from her own innocent horror at what The Beautiful Mother carried across the planks: the two shockingly red-haired, wrinkled, newborn faces peering out of the blankets along with their grasping threadlike fingers and their tiny fiddling pink and white nails.

With no small ambivalence Beatrice thought to leap away from her darling Grandmère into her little Mother's arms, but there they were: two infants where once she had lain not all that long ago, where once she had been sung to and had sung back in her own infant way.

"And what are your babies' names?" Grandmère asked in her warm manner. "The little red-haired things."

"Why, Raulf, of course, is the littler one," The Beautiful Mother replied. "And, Loup is the other, the one with the cute little mole on his throat."

To the littlest child there, even smaller than the newborn

babes, Grandmère cried, "Look! Here are your little long brothers! And, Grandpère," she said, tilting her head up to where thin Grandpère was towering over them and glowering in his clean white shirt and grey summer suit. Grandpère squinted at the babies again. "Grandpère—" Grandmère prodded. "Say you like them ever so much."

"Has either of them got a middle name?" Grandpère asked, thinking that one baby might have got one name at least similar to his.

"Yes," The Beautiful Mother said; and behind her, Papa G. rolled his eyes in anticipation of the explanation. "They're both middle-named Horton—because I like the sound of it," The Beautiful Mother said, rather haughtily, at which Beatrice felt a smile break out for the first time in a long while over her pale lips.

"Horton?" Grandmère and Grandpère cried at once.

"Are there Hortons then, on your side, Son?" Grandpère said to Papa G. who shook his elegant, neatly combed, dark head back and forth and shrugged up his arms.

"I think not," Papa G. smiled, shyly showing all his well-enameled teeth. Papa G. and The Beautiful Mother in their proud moment could not take their smiling eyes off one another.

"Both?" Grandmère said, shifting Beatrice to her other hip. "I don't get it."

"They're named after that new film star, the funny one,

the cartoon," The Beautiful Mother bragged. "Don't you get it? Together they're named after the same animal. They both mean wolf! I thought it would be cute since there were two."

It was the last time Beatrice ever recollected hearing The Beautiful Mother speaking in a self-explanatory and ingratiating tone. "Well," she snapped, then in quite another voice. "I don't expect there is much of a movie-going crowd out here. If I hadn't already sold the city house, I might consider this merely a vacation, the first half of a trip on the train, foreshortened—"

"Now now," Grandmère said to her grownup daughter. "You know your husband's lost his job; these are not the most regular of times." And it was true, it was the beginning of a depression. It was not the Great Depression, quite, but it would do until the next big one came along soon after.

"Claudette, Claudette," Uncle Thibault broke in, bouncing up and down on his toes on the brick platform. "It's me, your own Little Brother Thibault. Claudie, Claudie, here I am to say hello." This, too, was an exceptional memory—of recognizing her own Beautiful Mother as possessing the given name spoken out loud, and of Uncle Thibault standing on his own two feet and crying out in good cheer.

Grandpère coughed very quickly then, and gently, to remind Thibault of the tight control required in his case at public gatherings. At which, Uncle Thibault turned suddenly and with pronounced strides bore his long skinny body away from them through the cornfield. The assembled family looked to see Uncle Thibault wandering away along the railroad tracks. Like an exclamation point he seemed, on his tiny feet, speeding away down toward the intervening lane.

"Oh God," Grandmère sighed. "There off he goes. Off again. Grandpère, I wish you hadn't coughed at him. Whoever will bring him back now in all this heat?"

"I didn't cough at him," Grandpère offered, stroking back the strands of his silver hair at the top of his head. "I'm most sorry, Mame, but it wasn't my fault the boy ran off. I didn't cough."

"Now, Elvered," Grandmère said. "I know you wouldn't mean to—"

"'Twas a gnat," he said. "'Twas a gnat got inside. I am most powerfully sorry to have yawned and let the creature in while I was gawking at the new little flame-haired ones of bogus nomenclature—no disrespect to you, Claudette."

For The Beautiful Mother it would be impossible, if on principle only, to turn around and haul her bags back onto the locomotive. Still they all were beside her on the railway platform. It was impossible to retract her decision to move home with her parents now. The Beautiful Mother had never once changed her mind in her lifetime; and besides, this time she had sold her house back in the Territories.

Her lower lip went up and down as Grandpère went on about his astonishment at the children's names and Uncle Thibault transformed himself increasingly into a fly speck in the scene.

The Beautiful Mother went red and trembling, though silent still, looking down the tracks quite the other way as if she could jump back onto the locomotive that was now sealed and heaving itself noisily away.

"And for penance, Mame, for yawning at a bad joke that has got to be borne by our own living grandsons and their issue—for an eternity—a gnat dashed down between my capped teeth and got my goat real good. I just had to cough, Mame, or else I would have choked."

"There there, now, Father. Don't disturb yourself," Grandmère warned.

Beatrice had to lay her cheek right down affectionately on the large peony-flowered breast in gratitude for her gentle tone. Grandmère's Parisian perfume wafted up as soft as a cloud of baby powder and wreathed the miniature lady's apple-sized head. "I understand quite perfectly. You couldn't help yourself. It is a shock to all, of course. Now let's see to finding Thibault." Down the railroad tracks, quite opposite from the smoky wake of the departed train, Uncle Thibault was trundling, already a goodly distance away. "Best put your hat on, Elvered," Grandmère said, "lest you catch a stroke in this steam heat."

"And, how has Thibault been?" The Beautiful Mother asked of Grandmère curtly, jiggling the babies up and down. Ceremoniously, Papa G. held out his arms for one or the other tiny twin, but The Beautiful Mother had no desire to relinquish anything now that she was infuriated—and with everyone in sight. Papa G. slipped off then in a trail after Grandpère along a pair of disappearing tracks. One after the other they went, their hats bobbing up and down like bachelor's buttons on a dry prairie wind that lifted up the hems of their suit coats every so slightly as they went.

"Same as he ever was—" Grandmère said, "just Thibault."

Every now and then Grandpère could be heard gently calling out for him, "Thibault—it's time to go now. Let's turn around, Thibault. Come back and move along toward the car. Please don't make us go quite so far now. Be a good boy and come right back, won't you, Thibault. Be a good boy."

"Yes," Grandmère said to The Beautiful Mother. "Let's do head off to the car. Bring your little Mastrioni and your Raskolnikov, or whatever you've gone and named them now. Might as well be Patch and Pocket for the relevance to Grandpère's family. You know quite well that your father will call them Edgard and Renard after his brothers no matter what you call them. Well, let that be an end on it." Neither Grandmère nor The Beautiful Mother showed any signs of emotion now in their musculature, but for the one thing: The Beautiful Mother paled and bit down hard on her lip and nearly started to cry at this thought.

"We've got pan-fried chicken waiting to home," Grandmère went on mildly. "Just as you like, Claudette. And the potatoes will surely be waterlogged if we don't head back. We can run alongside the tracks in the car and pick the men up on the way."

For Beatrice it was an exciting day. Even though she had not yet been held by her own Beautiful Mother, she had set her eyes on the long-lost face and seen that The Beautiful Mother was just as lovely as anyone who had been restored from the dead could ever hope to be.

To her mother's credit, it was later remembered in the Book of Dreams that she actually did cry when Beatrice arrived at the big house, but only after Papa G. could not tear her away from Grandmère in order to be handed up to where The Beautiful Mother lay resting on the rose settee.

In the kitchen, smoothing down her own silver hair and then wiping hot streaks from Bea's face, Grandmère reassured her that she, her own Grandmère, would never once abandon her to another foreign land or give up interest in any pursuit or little whim she might take up. For Bea, the already aging Grandmère promised, she would be stability itself as long as she lived.

Sixteen years later, a horrible sound would come to them all early in July, the sound of millions of insects chewing in the fields. The villagers exclaimed that as of sunrise everything that should have been green had turned black and was undulating; and still the raucous sound of more locusts coming filled the sky. One by one, the locals entered Beatrice's chambers and could not speak, and what difference would it have made if they had spoken? Over the deafening sound, no one could have heard them anyway.

THE TWENTIETH DAY

Lessons in Breastfeeding

Bea remembered those early days very well. Everywhere on Grandmère's farm, the red-haired baby boys were exhibited at her mother's breasts, like twin tulips, sucking, sometimes simultaneously, through their individual straws. And during one night, in the middle of some childish and forgettable dream, already recumbent in the basket that would soon become her permanent home, a child of nearly three sat up to see the small beautiful Mother buttoning up one side of her dress and letting down the other to reveal her breast like a small white dimpled purse. The Beautiful Mother stood in the lamplight on her bedside chair and strained over the full size crib, exchanging them, one full-sized baby brother for the other.

In a wash of tears, Bea turned her back on them and sighed into her coverlet until, behind her, the back legs of the chair on which her mother stood let out a squeak and The Beautiful Mother emitted a cry of alarm. The Beautiful Mother fell straight over, half-dressed, into the crib between Loup and Raulf, crying out—My back, my back, and again: my back. Beatrice first rushed to the side of the crib. "Mama," Bea called from beneath the rungs of the side rails. "Mama, all right?"

"Stop crying," The Beautiful Mother rebuffed when she could catch her breath. "Go get Grandmère and, just once, think of someone besides yourself." In a moment, her grandparents and Papa G. had been summoned by the abashed child. And before long, Doctor Every had come to prescribe the heat and the liniment. But most importantly, he ordered the immediate weaning of the twins—with complete bed rest, sedatives, and a tightly bound chest for The Beautiful Lactating Mother. Formulas would be mixed and administered to the infants by Grandmère and neighborhood volunteers by day. At night Papa G. would be responsible should the infants wake.

In the formidable silence that comes over a house after sundown in deep country, for at least three weeks Bea pulled herself over the side of her basket, onto the polished surface of the mahogany table, then plummeted to the flowered rug, and—driven by some murmur or wafting maternal milky aroma—began her further descent as though into the well. Down the twisting narrow steps, clutching to the lip of each tread, Bea lowered herself until finally she stood at the bottom in the shadow of the kitchen door.

From this vantage point, she could see quite clearly through the crack: what went on in there on the living room floor. There on the supportive surface of Grandmère's thick maroon living room carpet, back and forth, The Beautiful Mother rolled in anguish. My back, she moaned. My back. Her flannel nightgown was open on one side, her breast red as a poppy at the tip, as she steered the terrible sucking Loup up to it. Raulf lay with his red hair aflame against her other side, already the more patient. For a moment there was an expression of pain on Mama's face and then a shudder went over her as she pulled Loup's lips away. She rested the back of her hand against her own forehead then and sighed, for once in her life seemingly at peace. With admiration and envy, adulation and hatred, Beatrice watched. Before her, her own mother reversed those twin usurpers and pressed her breasts simultaneously into their mouths..

By day, The Beautiful Mother continued to follow doctor's orders. She bound her breasts and slept. It was so easy to appease Dr. Every in his ordered bed rest—because by day she was completely exhausted after each strenuous night of sneak-nursing around and about the house. Beatrice opted to be up for sunrise breakfast and then to creep about as though nothing had happened, bearing her secret and growing paler yet dark as a raccoon around the eyes. In her doll-sized furniture and even at table, Bea fell asleep. So tired was she that on one occasion she fell from the little chair that had been set onto the end of the family table for her into the soup tureen, and had to be rescued by ladle. So it has been recounted by her loving but perhaps a bit zealous Aunt Burnoose to the village historian.

The reader will kindly note Beatrice's quick response as it was written in the margins:

I, Beatrice, myself do not recall, nor believe, that I have ever been small enough to have had to cling to a soup ladle for my salvation. It is only oral history related here; and, as we all know, the size of objects in a story is subject to affectionate distortions of imagination.

The ladle anecdote, representative of the nature of Beatrice 's family history, however, infiltrated village lore. Grandmère, so the children's story books and the village tour guides now report, showered her on that day kicking and wailing in the kitchen sink, then swaddled her in dishtowels and tucked her into the cradle that Papa G. had made for her birth in the Distant Territories. After this, Beatrice was ordered to bed for a designated period until she should regain her color and lose the owl-eyes. Soon that phase had crept into something like a year, and then time itself began again its gentle cascade.

TWENTY-ONE

Wrenching News

"There there," Dr. Every said to her on a later visit, administering a miniature mustard plaster to Beatrice's wheeze. "You are so close to your mama, even with your minuscule spirit, that you have taken to sleep-walking in her stead. Cover up now or you'll catch a terrible chill with that wet head. Dear dear, you are going to need your common sense with a pair of brothers about like that."

It was then that the doctor gave her what he considered to be the bad tidings about the Twins. One after the other the Twins had been squeezed out of The Tiny Beautiful Mother like toothpaste from a tube. The twins would not only always be tall—much taller than their older sister who had ceased to grow nearly at the moment she had been delivered, Dr. Every gently said but they might be even taller than their great-great-Grandpère, whom he himself could recall. They were also likely to be, just perhaps, a little simple-minded, Dr. Every had known this from the moment he'd first laid eyes on them. "It was a difficult birth," he said, "as your mother has described."

Never, during their lives, were the drinking habits of the Secret Nurslings divulged by Beatrice. Nor for that matter was it mentioned by any other family member who might also have wandered out of the bedroom for a drink of water, there to stand quietly with his little girl in the corner of the doorway watching the moonlight falling onto the living room rug where a mother caressed what she already knew to be her somewhat ill-fated boys. The last time Beatrice recalled seeing them nursing, the boys were fully four years old. At the time they were the oldest pupils in the kindergarten section of the one room school, a position they would have the honor of holding jointly for seven years and one make-up summer session.

TWENTY-TWO

A Horizontal View

The Year of Being Bed-fast soon enough arrived and passed for Beatrice, and then, too, a number of months flew by. Still no one reminded her, a little child, that it was time now to rise up. By the time Beatrice was to be released, her mother had been chasing about with the little boys out of doors for a season and a half. But then, that autumn, too, passed, and still Beatrice remained in the care of Grandmère, resting atop the bureau in her basket.

One day it was the doctor's orders keeping her to her basket, and the next it was merely habit and fear, one quite as powerful as the other, enforced by The Beautiful Mother even in the face of Grandmère's questions. On the part of the rest of the family, it was forgetfulness; and perhaps, they humbly admit to this day, a bit of hatefulness, too, at the child's refusal to be ordinary, at least in appearance.

TWENTY-THREE

And Swift for You...

It was a small county, of postage stamp size, Grandpère always said; and theirs was an even smaller town. On the peninsular northwest edge of it, blossomed their tiny farm right in the middle of the middlemost county of the middlemost state, if you left out the unfortunate purchase of Louisiana. In this territory, her skinny city father, freed from his governmental job, grew completely healthy, even brawny, in the more than pleasant country air, communing daily with the odors of cows and good corn. Even though in his life he had never raised more than two pigs, he liked to declare himself a pig farmer—as a political act, he touted.

Though Beatrice's father had not gained an ounce of aggression since he had settled into his in-law's house, he and they had agreed adamantly on this one point: when the time came, the Twins would be shipped off to a good Territorial university—whether the school would have them, they quipped, or not. The necessity of paying shipping fees for the Twins came increasingly into doubt. How peculiar that at their size and age they could not, in any language, easily read.

On Bea's higher education, no one seemed to agree. Grandmère was determined that Beatrice be treated just the same as if she had been as tall as anyone. To which, The Beautiful Mother said precisely, within hearing distance of half the locality: "Excuse me, but I am the child's mother. Short is one thing, girl is another; girls stay at home; boys, whatever their natures, go to University."

On her own, Beatrice had learned to read, leaning over the books in a basket at first and calling out whenever she wished to have a page turned. Perhaps predictably, Beatrice had especially enjoyed *Thumbelina, Giants and Dwarves, The Hunchback of Notre Dame, The Poor Little Rich Girl, Of Human Bondage, Toulouse the Great, The Metamorphosis, The Rise and Fall of the Roman Empire,* and *Don Quixote.*

"What is this?" The Beautiful Mother yelped, if she should find herself in the house when Bea called to Grandmère to have the giant pages turned. "Perhaps we should buy a set of fans and stand over you humming a tune?"

The Beautiful Mother had been educated in the best of private girls' schools where her friends had pulled that very fan trick on her—as a joke on her stiff attitude.

It was the difference in their heights that made the difference to The Beautiful Mother. While The Beautiful Mother was not officially considered a dwarf, Beatrice was—to use a euphemism—more than close. She was a full eight inches shorter than The Beautiful Mother.

Papa G. and Grandpère, true to their winter temperaments, said very little about their conflict. Nor did Grandpère say much in her defense. Yet, at night, she would find books from them propped beside her bed; and in them, daringly, the fly-leaves would be inscribed.

> *A good understanding of fossils will serve you well with your mother. You make me proud.*
>
> *Love, Papa G.*

And,

> *Swift for you, my little darling.*
> *Love,*
> *your doting Grandpère*

Soon she turned away from the elation of reading Swift's fictions yet another time. It was to his essays that now she turned, as she grew more famished. She saw now an irony even in the irony of Swift's prescribed menu.

TWENTY-FOUR

A Smelly Business

By the time Beatrice reached the middle of her fast, the Twins had already measured over seven feet three inches. They remained skinny, redheaded and freckled, gawky and silent, rarely saying a word to anyone except when angered, not even when addressed. The Twins had reached physical adolescence when they were six and a half years old. There they were: suddenly shot up tall, crackles like paint chips all through each voice. And, the spots on each face! Even before their eighth year they had seemed strange animals, new pets perhaps. Their manly forms had begun to come in; their legs were finely covered in lengths of soft copper hair. Their shoulders grew broad as lintels, yet their arms hung like individual strands of spaghetti from their furry pits. Yes, Grandmère and Bea projected: the Twins would be nearly ten-feet-four in height and twenty-four in age before the date of their graduation, not as tall as their Cousin Christopher, but tall, very tall, so it seemed.

In middle school, the Twins began to speak at length about everything round, not only things with wheels like motorcycles and cars, but also rounds of cheese, peas, oranges, apples, peaches, kiwi fruits, peasant bread. They ate only round things. Grandmère nearly went mad adhering to their round demands. It was only after Doctor Every lectured her on the consequences of letting already skinny boys go on hunger strikes in order to get round food that Grandmère began the round menu and stuck to it for nearly ten years. For a full year, the Twins refused to admit eggs to the menu.

"Nothing ever ovoid?" Grandmère begged.

"Why, they are purists!" Sister Beatrice sister tried to explain, for once siding with her brothers.

Not long after they had begun their thoroughly round menu, the force of 'The Round' also led them to go out on tandem dates, seeking out round things, or so they said. They particularly liked nice round mouths and breasts and bottoms, they said, and a perfectly round kiss to be placed roundly on a juicy mouth.

"My," Bea said with deep affection, recalling it with her grandmother—"I did have such a keen heart for them then—watching them getting ready to go out. I remember the day I said to them: 'Aren't you two a sight?'" She was amazed that the Twins heard no warmth from her in this innocuous phrase. Out they rushed in a huff, faces and hair ablaze, leaving her in her usual corner to stare out through the latticework of her confinement at all their roundly balled up, dirty socks.

So it is with adolescents, she said to comfort herself, as everyone who is already even nearly grown up fully knows.

Sometimes when the whole family was gathered, Beatrice would stare at them in a game without ever turning; and they could not, without being obvious, turn back to stare at her. Each boy's bowler sat on his right knee and jumped up and down with every bounce of his feet. Awkwardly they ate, increasingly self-conscious, lifting circular pasta bits out of their pastel bowls and spilling them out of their trembling round soup spoons. Down the front of their shirts, it flowed, leaving circular ornaments among their buttons as their bodies reddened like Christmas tapers from neck to brow.

"Evil eye!" they screeched then. "Evil eye, don't look at us!"

The Twins had traveled through the first oval together in birth and now they continued in each other's company looking for potential wives. Now, even as one was showering, the other would sit on the closed lid of the toilet and wait for his brother to step out, all the while calling names of all the girls who might be possibilities, back and forth. They dressed alike but for one thing—one wore a navy blue bandana around his neck, the other wore one circling his head as they had seen in their pirate books.

TWENTY-FIVE

Their Usual Props

While waiting—for what Beatrice didn't quite know—she spent part of each day propped up on the *Volume Library* or on her old donated home-schooling books. There she sewed at the black-and-gold scrolled toy machine on the little stand Papa G. had designed to rest over the edge of a packing crate. She had, with considerable effort, learned by now to sit up for quite long periods of time, her grandmother often reminded her mother. This in itself was a triumph, Grandmère said.

"Trying to make something of yourself at last!" The Beautiful Mother laughed, perhaps jealously, whenever Bea started up the small black wheels and the needle began rapidly to go in and out of the dresses she made lovingly now for her grandmother, and for anyone who asked. She had made only one sundress for her mother who had been only momentarily impressed. Now the fabric swam around Beatrice in the illustrious sea of her further bed linens.

"No thanks to you," Beatrice snapped unwisely. "If you hadn't been denying that you are so short yourself, you wouldn't have inclined to cast me out, and at a primary moment in my development—"

"Now hush," Grandmère said. "We all have our own ways—although some are more responsible and more kindly than some others are— Isn't that the way?"

The Beautiful Mother huffed and returned to her scrabble board whereupon she was making Papa G. suffer immensely and publicly. "You are oblivious to everything," The Beautiful Mother said to Beatrice, having made a very fine word on the board. Papa G. threw his hat in the air and howled in mock agony. "For instance," she revealed vindictively, "I don't suppose you realize that your brothers are at this very moment hired out on the back of someone else's truck to detassel corn in the boiling heat."

"Why no," Beatrice said. "I thought that's what they wanted. No one ever tells me a thing."

"You never listen," The Beautiful Mother said. "You have always got your face in a book, but then how could you listen to the stuff of life—for instance that your brothers are working 12 to 14 hours a day in the boiling sun to save us?"

"You said that," Beatrice said. "About the sun, I mean."

"Yes indeed," The Beautiful Mother said. "And there you have it," she said to Papa G in triumph. "I've managed to use a QU as well as a Z. Whatever will I think of next?"

"But why have they hired out to someone else?" Beatrice asked, burrowing with her needle into the hem, riding the internal roll of a fabric wave. "Why aren't they detasseling our own corn?"

"Shush," Grandmère coaxed. "You'd better shush now."

Her mother made a rude sound with her lips, completely uncharacteristically. "Well you might ask, Miss Bassinet of the World! What's happened to our own corn—"

"Now, Claudette," Grandmère said. "You can't expect the child to know what goes on in the world if you don't tell her straight out. You've made a point of not telling her, in fact. —Of not even carrying her outside, all because of your own pride and embarrassment."

"Why should we tell her?" the Mother huffed. "Tell her? What can she do about anything? She never even learned to walk."

"I did, too, learn to walk. Aunt Burnoose says—"

"All right, all right," The Beautiful Mother said. "You learned to walk. You just didn't stick to it. You grew bored with walking or something. You gave it up. Walking, I mean, for seventh heaven."

"Tell me immediately!" Beatrice cried out. "I am part of this family. Why are the boys working for somebody else?"

"Because the crop is dead, that's why," The Beautiful Mother yelled. "We stand to lose the farm, that's why. I don't suppose you realize that while you've been holed up in here we've had a drought and then a flood in one season. Half the county's under water, the other half is dry as a bone. We—

just lucky as we infinitely are—also have the extraordinary luck of having a dwarf living with us—so we got both the drought and the flood!"

"Oh," Beatrice said. "No one's told me," she said. "How very strange."

"Yes, how very strange," The Beautiful Mother said rather snippily.

"All anyone wanted to talk about when they came to me was their family troubles and love. No one said a thing about crops or floods."

"That's all that's left to talk about, that's why, you ape," The Beautiful Mother said. "All we've got now is God and love and a pile of dirt or mud."

"But Papa G.," she asked. "Why didn't you tell me?"

Papa G. was studying the scrabble board intensely. "Didn't want to worry you, Sweets," he said without looking up. "You have enough to worry about as it is."

"Papa!" The Beautiful Mother said, for her mate had scored a very good word.

He smiled almost beatifically then. Beatrice saw that he had gone considerably grey since she had last noticed his hair toward the beginning of the past week.

"Don't you worry," Papa G. comforted. "I've got a scheme. That Adam Baum won't be taking over our house with his chained roosters and his artificially fertile hens. Now he's got everybody who once was his own proud self, working slave labor for him, if they don't want to starve—"

"Why, Papa—" The Beautiful Mother said, "I believe you've led me to an idea I wouldn't ordinarily have."

"Just play, Mama," Papa G. said. "I think I'm bound to beat you just this once. Don't spoil it with schemes against nature. Nature will do what it will. I will take care of the rest."

When the boys came home that night they were in an odd kind of exhausted ecstasy. Somehow they had both in the same day passed a pop quiz. Loup actually picked Beatrice up out of her cradle and held her high over his head, turning her carefully round and round, passing her back and forth with Raulf who whisked her from door to cornice and back again, her feet kicking and her dark hair streaming out behind. "Star-nosed moles fly overhead the dead," Loup laughed, quoting that Richard Wilbur poem he had so often liked to hear her recite for him when he was yet a young boy.

"Don't you laugh at that," Beatrice said. "And put me down! Have you both gone off your heads?"

"I'm not laughing at it!" Loup cried out; and for just that once, she could see that she had once upon a time touched him very deeply with something that had affected her.

Before Beatrice knew it, a pen was coming toward her and, in a flash, Raulf had drawn a star in indelible ink at the tip of her nose. "Want us to recite the whole thing?" Loup dared, wiggling his blond eyebrows and showing his gums.

"No," Beatrice pouted. "I know that poem. I taught it to you." Whenever Beatrice felt the need, she had quoted that poem in her Book of Dreams. It was so beautiful, she thought, that she needed to put it in everything. Weren't we all nearly the same height underground in our final rest—in the end—weren't we all merely star-gazing at star-nosed moles flying overhead or among the dead?

Bea stared down Loup's outstretched arms at all his silky yet thick, straight, glossy, red hairs. They looked like the copper filaments at the center of those long black wires her father had taken to winding at night among various, smooth, red strings of dynamite.

"Put me down!" she said.

"Put me down at once!" the twin boys mocked, laughing aloud, spinning her round and round and back and forth between them near the ceiling beams.

"Wow, you are light as quills!" Raulf said.

"This one's not eating us out of house and home," Loup squealed.

"Put me down," she yelped. "Put me in my crib!"

Just then, Loup stopped short with his sister held in a flying pattern near the chandelier. "Raulf, what is that?" he gasped. A ridge of darkness had entered under the door.

"Good Heavens!" Grandmère said and took up the

broom. Raulf was forced to hold the dustpan. But when the dust was in the receptacle, the vision of darkness entered again.

"Oh no," Grandpère said and buried his head in his sleeve. Soon he had begun to sob, and even Grandmère and Papa G. could not think what to say.

"It's only dirt," Loup said, bringing Beatrice down from his shoulder to perch on the increasingly dusty mantle next to a portrait of Irish cliffs.

"No, by God, it's not 'only dirt.'" Grandpère squeaked. "It's your family's topsoil, that's what it is!"

They all looked at it, so seemingly fine, coming in at the closed windows and especially under and around the door, the rest blowing off perhaps to the Territorial Coast or some place where they didn't need soil or money, or so it seemed.

Loup brought her back down from the mantle and sat her on his knee. They were like a theatre audience then, watching a very sad play. Slowly it crept in on them. The line grew large again, and Grandmère barefoot and vigilant in the blue flowered house dress Bea had made for her, swept it away. Again it appeared; this time, Raulf swore, it had many sets of tiny eyes in it, like newts looking out.

"Stop it, Raulf!" Loup demanded, "Don't get bat crazy on us. Besides you'll drive the Midgie mad."

"Light the candle," The Beautiful Mother said.

"No, don't," Grandmère said. "The wind has swept

entirely in here now. You'll burn us down. Look at the curtains." They were nearly horizontal to the floor with the wind beastly and howling under them.

"Burn us down then!" Grandpère screeched. "What good is anything to us now?"

"Now there, now there," Grandmère tried to reassure. They sat in the dark with wet towels over their mouths while the grit began to cover them.

"Now there," Grandmère said. "Beabones will offer up a prayer."

"Dear God, we pray for deliverance from filth!" Beatrice coughed, clinging to Loup's buttons.

"What kind of prayer is that?" The Beautiful Mother snapped from her rocking chair. She could no longer see her games or her book.

"Don't get nasty now, Mother," Papa G. said sweetly. "You know that, anyways, I was winning. I should be the peevish one."

"We are being buried alive!" Grandpère cried in an eerie voice. The walls rattled around, and outside a hideous noise rose up much like that of the 6:05 locomotive.

"Don't let them in!" Grandpère screamed.

Grandmère threw herself onto his lap and flung a towel over both of their heads.

"What is it?" Beatrice called out from where she had been tucked under Loup's t-shirt. "What is that dreadful, grinding sound?"

"Don't even bother explaining it to her, Loup," Raulf said. "She doesn't even know what a hamster is."

For the first time in as long as Beatrice could remember, no one laughed at the mention of that word.

"Those is locusts," Uncle Thibault quietly said from the corner where he had been sitting all afternoon unnoticed, perched on the floorboards like a praying mantis. "They is eating everything in sight!"

"That is just about right—for my life anyways," Grandpère sobbed. "I've got bugs that will eat anything and a granddaughter who wants to starve to death. Now I've got to see my whole family buried alive without ever we leave the house."

"There there now," Immense Grandmère said.

"Check its size, Raulf," Loup called out in the gritty gloom.

Beatrice heard him crawl across the floor.

"Wee doggies!" Raulf said. "It's everywhere, and it's one whip big!"

"Don't you worry, Grandpère. Loup, give me your shirt and the Midgie."

Suddenly Beatrice felt exposed though in the interior dusk she could see very little. The two brothers wound their shirts together around her then entirely. "Why thank you, brothers," she said. "I thank you for your kindness."

"And we thank you, Midgie," Raulf said, laying Beatrice down, full length, along the bottom of the door to stop up the crack where the dirt swept in.

"Oh my goodness," was all Beatrice could think to say as she lay there.

The wind continued to howl and the flying dirt and locusts grated like sandpaper all around the outer edges of their home, grinding away at everything, as they would see in the morning when they tried to look out through their permanently frosted windows. Before long the family had managed to rejoice in a song or two and then just as abruptly they had finished their singing. For the first time, Beatrice thought while lying at the foot of the door like a papoose, all members of the family, but for herself, were neatly tucked at the very same time into their own beds and Uncle Thibault was passed out on the sofa. The dwarf could detect little or no snoring, whether because of the overriding sound of the storm of wind and insects, or because of their new-found inner tranquility.

TWENTY-SIX

Grandmère Takes a Notion

Several weeks later, after the house had been swept and even shoveled out from top to bottom, Beatrice looked up from her knitting to notice that the men and boys had gone off to work the fields and The Beautiful Mother had fallen asleep in the heat over her afternoon game of solitaire. Stout Grandmère came to the side of her basket. She was wearing Beatrice's favorite house dress, the one Beatrice had made for her with the miniature pink and yellow roses sprinkled all over a white field.

"Short Stuff," Grandmère began, oddly enough, in a lecture, "your Mama may have abandoned you for ten and a half weeks while you were an infant, but that is no reason for you to abandon faith in yourself and in your good looks, which as you know utterly everyone remarks upon. It's time," she said "for you to take upon yourself the duty of establishing a flirtation. Besides," she said, whispering and looking very pale, "I'm beginning to be concerned about your well-being here. Well, let's not talk about that. Let's look on the bright side and find you some quick alternatives."

Beatrice was not afraid to say, straight out to her grandmother, that she did not feel she would be very good at choosing men, for all her lack of experience. But her grandmother said that soon enough she would find that it was much simpler to attract them than to like them. No sooner had Grandmère put the ad in the Monday night paper saying that Beatrice would receive courtiers on Wednesday, than a line of circus owners, young and old farm-grown men, and the local egg-packing boys began to form at the side of the house. The ad read:

Very tiny young woman, 3'1" tall, sweet, kind, wise, devoted, knowledgeable, seeks marriageable mate of similar disposition. Height of no concern.

The line of men continued, so Beatrice was told by her suddenly interested Mother, well past the back of the barn—not nearly so far as the Sunday lineup for her advice, but substantial to be sure. Nevertheless, as the men gathered, minute by minute by minute by minute her grandmother's health seemed to turn for the worse. A pallor seemed to overtake her spirit as well, when each time The Beautiful Mother went light-heartedly to look out between the ruffled window curtains. Occasionally she would even throw open the front door to glimpse the well-tanned men waving and ingratiating themselves.

"That's not what I had in mind, Claudette! You know it isn't. It's horrific that you even think of it!" Grandmère shouted when the door was pulled tight shut again.

"Still, all in all," The Beautiful Mother said. "You have to admit, it's not a bad idea."

"It's an irresponsible idea!" Grandmère howled. " And immoral! You know that's not the sort of ad I put in. As long as I'm alive there'll be no such thing in my house, not to our little girl. It's reprehensible! And! It's a sin!" Grandmère put a hand on Beatrice forehead and then her other hand was steadying itself abruptly on the back of the bedside chair.

"Well," Beatrice's mother said. "Would you rather starve to death? Look in the pantry."

"What is it, Mother?" Beatrice asked. "What's the matter with Grandmère, and whatever does she mean?"

"You'd better lie down now, Mother," The Beautiful Mother said, brushing by Beatrice's basket to attend to her own faltering maternal dignitary. "You mustn't get so het up. You will give yourself a stroke."

The Immense Grandmère sat down with a jolt and put her silver head in both hands. The dwarf could see the bun at the back of her grandmother's head bobbing up and down, strangely shuddering.

Perhaps Grandmère had anticipated her lingering illness when she set out to place Beatrice in another location. Too soon Grandmère was taken ill and was retired into the other room. Beatrice could not understand it. Her mother then— instead of worrying and pining—took on new force.

Moving down the line across the backyard, clipboard in hand, Beatrice 's mother took down the name of every marriage applicant. Past the hen house where Uncle Thibault lived and then Rude Raoul's empty doghouse, into the cool shadow of the barn, she seemed to float in her new determination. "For future reference," she said, "I'll take your addresses as well." Beatrice could see her in the reflection that Cousin Christopher's mirror had given her through her window. Her mother was speaking politely with each of them and turning the pages of her calendar. When she came into the house at last, she said she had made her selection.

"For what?" Beatrice asked, sitting upright. "Selection for what?" Grandmère moaned in the back room, nearly comatose.

"I have seriously considered all the applicants," The Beautiful Mother replied, exceedingly cheerful, brushing out her own thick brown hair with a silver brush in front of Beatrice's basket. "I have named one Adam Baum, owner of the local Egg Factory, the winner. He is a slender man with no hips, no shoulders, and no beard. He has a good head of hair and a pointy chin. Even he didn't mind waiting in line for over an hour. And, he holds a prominent place in society."

Grandmère gulped in the backroom and the bed springs creaked but Grandmère did not appear at Beatrice's basket.

"For what?" Beatrice cried. "The winner of what?"
"For you! You idiot!" Beatrice's mother shouted.
"For me?" Beatrice exclaimed.
"He is more than noteworthy," she said. "He will treat you well—as you deserve. And besides—"
"Besides what? Mother?" Beatrice screeched. "What will he want me to do? Have you gotten me a job in the egg factory? I could look by candlelight through eggs and see if they are fertile—"
"It's time you came of age," she said. "It's time you got out of that bin and pitched in for once. And besides," she said again, "Adam Baum holds the note on this farm. At any point he could turn us all into chicken ranchers. And his is not normal chicken-ranching, his chickens are in crates permanently. It's immoral. Because of you, he's holding off on ejecting us. Because of you we have another chance."
"Because of me what?" Beatrice shouted.
"Just because of you—" she whispered. "It is a matter far too delicate for mothers and daughters. You will have to speak to your brothers about that. They're younger and more worldly. Ask them what we have in mind for you."

TWENTY-SEVEN

A Beautiful Mother Takes the Upper Hand

So it all came out: According to Beatrice's brothers, who lived now in fear of their reputations being destroyed in the light of their mother's scheme, behind the barn Adam Baum had drawn Beatrice's mother and her clipboard to one side and had given her mother sixty dollars for next Thursday night.

"What do you mean a night with me?" Beatrice cried then and again to her mother later that day. "You're not allowing him to take me out of my basket? Not out of this house, Mother? Not that man you hate. Not Adam Baum?"

From the furthest bedroom came the sound of Beatrice's devoted Grandmère trying unsuccessfully to come to her.

"Now lie back, Mother, and rest," The Beautiful Mother called toward Grandmère's room.

"Of course not," The Beautiful Mother curtly answered Beatrice. "We might never get you back. And I begin to see that we might need you now. You've never been out of the house, you might die like a worm in the light, you poor unfortunate."

"But what does a night with me mean?" Beatrice inquired with no small amount of anguish, beginning to get an unseemly picture.

"It means the bean crop and the corn crop did not come in. You won't eat. We're hungry. Everyone else around here works, it's time you did."

"But what could I do? I could take in sewing."

"It's too slow. As I've said before, many times," The Beautiful Mother said coldly, "you could charge for your lordly advice to the lowly populace. How about that?"

Beatrice peered up at her rose-lipped mother mortified, as if she had never heard the suggestion before. "Charge for kindness? For a few sweet words? I will never ever do that, Mother. You can torture me before I will ever do that."

In the back bedroom Beatrice could hear Grandmère careening into unconsciousness.

"Whatever it means, I'm sure it will be unique," her mother said. "We've chosen the smallest and richest man in town for you. Take heart. I've arranged for the boys to go into town for the night so as to assure some privacy for them."

"Privacy for them?"

"For the boys. They are a little uncomfortable with the whole idea. You wouldn't want to taint their innocence. They are, after all, rather younger than you are."

"Only a month and two years."

"Don't start up again, I'm warning you, Beatrice,"

"But isn't Adam Baum that perverse man you always talk about, the owner of the egg factory, the one who's buying out all the neighbors' farms for poultry ranches?"

"I get the feeling you've begun to listen. The very self-same man," The Beautiful Mother said. "Now that your grandmother is feeling ill, I thought it time I took a hand in running things. Mr. Baum is well known in these parts. We thought enough of him to remortgage our farm with him, didn't we? We wouldn't give our money to anyone we didn't respect. And Mr. Baum surely would be a good friend to you. As I've just said, if you can remember back that far, he holds our mortgage. Who knows, he might even decide to marry you, he's nearly short enough."

"Marry me? I don't want to get married to anyone."

"Don't be so selfish, Miss Bea, and don't jump to conclusions. Who said he'd care for the likes of you anyway? Mr. Baum is a seasoned bachelor sort. I doubt he's interested in innocence and philosophy. Anyway we can only try. Your grandmother isn't able to take care of you, and you don't think I'm going to sit around here washing your hair and feet?" They both now usually wore their hair braided onto the backs of their heads like Grandmère, in giant chignons, and on her cheeks Beatrice wore a faint touch of rouge with the delicate scent of country roses, once applied by Grandmère.

The Beautiful Mother merely sighed when Beatrice asked what "bachelor sort" in that context might mean. Perhaps Beatrice's blue eyes actually rolled in terror. "You've already said 'yes' for me? Whatever shall I do?"

"That's easy," her mother laughed in her full-throated way, her blue topaz eyes luminous in her head.

"Don't act like a dwarf, or he'll think you're a fool. My advice to you for the rest of your life, concerning men, is to act intelligent. The rest of the women have been given stature greater than yours and have to diminish themselves so as not to seem fierce and threatening in the company of men. Men are skittish, Beatrice; when they are frightened they lose their physical powers, and that in itself makes them practically useless at even the simplest tasks. You, even more than I, have the good fortune of being so small that you can look sharp without being threatening. You've no need for lisping or catering to anyone, man or dog. You will never frighten a man enough so that he loses his power to make love or money. Why do you think so many men are interested in standing there behind the house in hopes of seeing you?"

"Make love?" Beatrice asked, but her Mama had grown hard as metal. Beatrice's mother's hair fell out of their hairpins in sable waves around her pretty doll face, her blue eyes gleamed gracefully out under the dark curved lashes.

"That means: No toying or prancing around. Tell him

exactly what you think."

"What if I don't know what I think? And, what does that mean they might lose the power? I don't understand any of it."

"Good lord," The Beautiful Mother said, plunking herself down on her own kitchen chair that Raulf and Loup had made to fit her. "You are nineteen going on twenty-four years old and you don't know anything. I should have expected it, with you running around in a basket all this time, with nothing for company but a pair of seventeen-year-old brothers and a doting old woman who would do anything for you. You've been stunted in your growth."

"Yes," Beatrice said. "If only I'd had the proper attention of a mother—"

"Don't give me that abandonment story again," her mother snapped. "If you were a normal human being, I'd have you run that tea in to your grandmother and take several biscuits with it. If you were a normal human being with half a heart, you'd be sitting there beside her bed, after all she's done for you. As it is, she will have to do it herself. I don't mind saying to you, I am getting concerned about Grandmère's health. Her own weight seems to have dropped down while you've been playing that ridiculous fasting game. Just think of this, Miss Bea, who—you might rightfully ask—will take care of the One Who Sleeps in Baskets, if anything permanently happens to the Immense

Grandmère? Today Uncle Thibault will be in to give you your bath. You may as well strip down."

"Uncle Thibault?!"

Beatrice began to cry suddenly then, and sob, and beg. It was something she had never done before, and she could not say exactly why she was doing it now, except for an unspeakable fear she had, based upon nothing but suspicion—or so The Beautiful Mother said again and again, in different phrases with noticeable frostiness. She didn't mind shaking her beautifully manicured pale-pink fingernail in Bea's direction.

"Well, you and Thibault are the only two who do nothing around here. You are the most freakish of the group. I think you'd do well to spend more time together. It might even be good to have you move out to the cabin with him where he can look after you properly. You can greet your visitors there. Surely Thibault can do that much for us. Times are difficult. But I don't suppose you'd have any sense of that, would you? Maybe you and Thibault could give each other a sense of purpose in life." She stuck her hands to her hips.

"For heaven's sake," she continued, "stop sobbing and retching. You are turning yourself an ugly red. Just this once, maybe I'd better bathe you before Mr. Baum comes to call on you. Maybe this creature will like you at once, and the entire day will be saved. Stop crying," she said again. "That other is only a back up plan."

"But what do you mean—for a night?" Bea cried out again as she took shelter from her, pulling her blanket up over her head.

Beatrice sputtered, trying hard to get better control over her thoughts so that she could hear what her mother said. Already she could tell quite clearly that Mr. Baum, whoever he was, was the preferable alternative to Uncle Thibault.

"Oh don't worry, it's not really just for a night. We wouldn't sell you off to just anyone who comes along. If he likes you, he has exclusive rights; but you are to remain here, at home, with us, where you belong. Thibault can see to you. Exclusive rights means: behave yourself, drink your tea and make conversation. Be pleasant or we will all be out on the street. Grandmère, too. We haven't got the money now even to call that buffoon Dr. Every for her. Well, maybe you can change all that if you work fast enough. I said, *Strip down and stop your blubbering!*"

TWENTY-EIGHT

A Little Lady's Unpleasant Memory

Memory and invention cannot always be pleasant, even for a primordial dwarf with a life no larger than a basket. On the twenty-eighth day of her fast, in a flood of tears and visions—partially instigated by waiting indefinitely for the newly discovered Cousin Christopher to return—the dwarfed icon was handed over to the most hateful of all her neighbors and her virginity extracted. After this indignity she felt she would never move again. She did not care to. While the pain itself was abundant, as she was told it must be for all women, even for those who were more suitably built for intercourse and childbearing, the pain was not so fierce as it might have been if her egg-farming courtier had been of enhanced proportions. "Why, more than half the women of this earth," her mother told her, "are forced to have intercourse with men they haven't chosen. Settle down and stop that whining."

She was offered many sweet and pungent tidbits, one by one, and even sugar petals by the man himself, but she would not break her fast for him. Time carried her back and forth in its dreamy arms now. She was a tiny terrifying thing, growing even tinier.

To whom would it matter what would come next? This she thought, again and again trying to comfort herself as she drifted off to sleep. But, of course, it did matter. Perhaps her visions of Cousin Christopher would comfort her. Her body wept through every pore. Why would her beloved Cousin not take her magic touch? And what was this fruit he had spoken of so quietly? No, she could not think of what had happened on that day, she would have to save it for another time, if that time of mental endurance ever came to her. She hoped sincerely that it would not.

TWENTY-NINE

The Limping Lady

On the twenty-ninth day, a woman came to her; and, although it was not unusual, it was this visit she chose not to forget. Beatrice had been dreaming of sitting on a riverbank, when who should appear but this young limping woman with a scar down her leg and the slightly muscular torso of one who must constantly bear the weight of a body brace.

Beatrice had found over her teenage years and even in her middle childhood that persons had come to her for advice, not merely to touch her forehead for luck and convocations. It was advice Beatrice thought that The Limping Woman sought. Together they sat, Bea in the lingering days of her fast, seemingly on the edge of the riverbank, and The Limping Woman on the edge of Beatrice's new wing chair, a gift from Adam Baum on the day of the consummation of their engagement. Indeed, it was in that very wingchair that Beatrice had been ceremoniously deflowered. Now the peculiar woman sat in it beside Beatrice where she lay in her newly decorated basket on the desk.

"The water is lovely today," Beatrice ventured. "I have not seen it so clear."

"Water?" asked the woman who felt stronger now, as she could not limp while sitting down.

"Yes, for some, water can be very clear."

Miraculously, The Immense Grandmère had risen from her bed on the night before; and, though she seemed to walk in a trance, she came in and placed a cool towel on Beatrice's head as though she, The Grandmère, had never taken ill. Humming a melancholy tune, she arranged the glossy white hydrangeas a deaf woman had brought in a yellow vase. The luscious flowers hung down now over her as though Bea herself had been laid out as an infant outside on the eastern slope beneath the giant tree hydrangea she remembered from the all too brief pedestrian period of her youth. There the land swooped up to a precipice of floral activity and overlooked the chicken pen where the resident fox had once come up to her and licked her arm affectionately.

"I see that you have a limp," Beatrice said to her when they had stopped admiring the flowers. "Would you care to tell me the story of your limp?"

"Yes," The Limping Woman said. "It was a holiday," she said, "and my children and I were in costume for a party. We were dressed as animals. My two sons were dressed as bears, and my daughter was a kangaroo."

"And you?" Beatrice asked.

"I was dressed as an ox."

"How did you choose what you wore?" Beatrice asked.

"My second child wore the bear suit because he wanted to look like his teddy bear. My little one wore a bear suit, but of another color, because he admires his brother. My daughter wore the kangaroo suit because it has a pocket and she could carry her doll."

"And yourself?"

"I wore the suit of the ox because my children thought it beautiful with my hair although my hair itself was covered. And it was reassuring to them, they said. You see my husband had just left me for another woman, who was not even very nice or attractive. We'd all thought we'd been very happy. We felt alone—even though there were four of us left and we were all very much in love with one another. Still, we missed the other one—my husband, their father. He had moved that week in with the other woman and her children. He was taking her children to the festival, we had heard. We were not even sure we wanted to go now, for fear that we would see them."

"But still you decided to go and make the best of it, even have a little fun. Was that it?"

"Yes," the woman with the limp said. "And then I got the limp. That's why I came to you, I don't know what to do."

"Maybe you should tell me now what it is you wanted to tell."

"Yes," she said looking miserable and relieved all at once. Pretty and sweet, she was, a tiny woman, relative to most of her gender, a bit stringy-haired, Beatrice noticed.

"I think I'm ready to hear it," Beatrice said, "although I can't be sure.'

"I don't like to talk about it," the woman with the limp said.

"I see that," Beatrice said. "Better do it though, since that's why you came."

"All right," she said. She lay her brown head down beside the basket and stared up at Beatrice who was looking over the side.

"I was run over with a car that night when we crossed the street. Three times."

"Three times!?"

"Yes, he went over me the first time and then he backed over me and then went forward over me again."

"In front of your children!" Beatrice exclaimed. It was not a question, but she could not help saying it. In spite of herself, Beatrice looked at the woman, with horror in her elfin face.

"Yes."

"Was it an accident and the driver panicked? Or, was it intentional?"

The Limping Woman could not lift her head. "It took me eight months in hospital, and then the nursing home.

But, he did not get my head under the wheels. That was one thing."

The Dwarf was just able to touch the tip of the woman's ear—if she leaned very hard against the rough edge of her basket. "Someone hired the driver to do this to you?"

"He was in jail for two months and then he had enough money to go back to another part of the world. I recognized him from the corner grocery in the interim. The children pretended to many that I was staying at home so that no one would take and separate them. They had to take care of one another. I don't know how they did it."

"Would you mind bringing me a cup of water please?" Beatrice asked. "Today I seem to have water on the brain."

"My problem is two-fold," The Limping Woman said, delivering the glass. "I can't get the sounds of my children's screams out of my head—And," she blurted it out, "my children are always afraid something will happen to me, or to one of us. They are always fearful."

"I can understand that," Beatrice said. "I was once merely stroking a bumblebee when I fell into a ditch and was pierced by the thorns of a rose." She held up her hands and The Limping Woman gasped to see the two stars in Beatrice's palms. The Limping Woman wrapped her hands around the glass and gulped the other half of Beatrice's water down. "I only mention it," Beatrice said, "because I was expecting to be stung by a bee I had befriended and I was harmed by something I thought harmless and beautiful."

"But it's your palms," The Limping Woman said. "It looks like—"

"I know what it looks like," Beatrice said, ever so gently. "But I will be the first to tell you that it was merely a rose bush. Maybe I should have a doctor try to fix them back to normal again. It would be painful but they would look fine."

"Oh, no!" cried The Limping Woman. "How could you think of removing them! Why! Don't you see what they are?"

"Oh, that is merely foolishness," Beatrice said. "I merely fell onto a rose bush."

"You were pierced by thorns!" the woman cried, aghast. "You must promise me never to have those scars removed! May I touch them?"

"Yes, of course," Beatrice said, "if you will promise me one thing!"

"Anything!" the sweetly limping lady said.

"Promise me you will hang the head of your oxen costume over your fireplace. And, everyday you must smile at it lovingly, especially when your children can see you. You still have the head, I think."

"Yes, I never wanted to see it again, so I could not bring myself to open the plastic bag that came from the hospital. The head is in that bag; it went with me in the ambulance."

"I thought as much," Beatrice said.

"You did?" The sweet limping lady now revealed that

she had very large brown eyes.

"Yes, I suspected it."

"You want me to hang that thing over my fireplace?" She seemed surprised but not annoyed with Beatrice. "All the time? After what has happened?"

"Yes," Beatrice said, "and you are to say to your children why you are doing it."

"Why am I doing it?" The Limping Lady asked in astonishment. "Of course, I will. But I can't see why—I'm sorry."

"Because without it, surely that auto would have found your own head. Your children chose your costume, and that costume confused your assailant and saved your life."

"Yes," The Limping Lady sighed. "I see now. I will hang that stuffed head over my fireplace."

"One more thing," Beatrice said.

"Yes, anything," The Limping Lady replied.

"Tell your children that every time you limp, it reminds you how they saved your life and how much you adore their every breath."

"Oh, I will!" The Limping Lady cried out. And then she sat down in a slump again and nearly burst into tears. She hung her head over Beatrice. "But what if he wants to do it again!"

"Move near the water as soon as possible," Beatrice said, "and never ever ask him into your new home. Always take the children outside to meet him when he comes to visit them. Never tell him anything at all about yourself. Not the slightest thing. Act as though he is the postman to whom you've never spoken but to say good-day."

"That's all?"

"Yes," Beatrice said.

"May I now?"

"If you wish," Beatrice shrugged, holding out her miniature palms and rolling her eyes back in her head.

III

Even before the Book of Dreams, came the dream itself, which may have been the living thing or may have not. In and out, it was woven like the many strands of the diminutive basket in which Beatrice, for most of her life, had lived.

On the night of weeping, on that advanced thirtieth day of her fast toward sainthood, she heard a voice narrating her dream, and it seemed to her that it was equally her voice and one from far away that called out to her when it said:

I am trying to think how I must have looked to him that day when I saw myself standing on the shore, a minuscule young woman intently listening, idle on the yellow sand in my riding clothes: royal blue they were, my usual riding jacket and pants, my honey curls tied up and bobbing down behind my head. My Great Dane stood at my side. It was an ordinary summer day. I waved and called toward the little boat cutting across blue waves.

In real life she tossed and turned in the yellow basket, dreaming intermittently. That evening The Beautiful

Mother scrubbed her very roughly and left her to dry in a damp nightgown with no coverlet. The fire that her newly speechless Grandmère had made early that morning before retiring again to her sick bed had nearly gone out. Back and forth, Beatrice tossed in the dream. Her own life was rather peculiar, even for a dwarf, she was thinking. It was not about Adam Baum she dreamed.

The day she met The Mild One he had been fishing off the side of a small, red, sailing boat. It was a day boat made of wood; it had no cabin on it. A single sail was all he had. He was sitting down, tacking back and forth, one hand on both rudder and mainsheet, the other pulling the net in. She saw The Mild One from that distance: his hair stood out like fingers of fire all over his head. His eyes were all one color, as if he had no pupils. She wanted to touch his hands. He was clean-shaven—but his hair was disheveled. Yes, his hair was very long and sunny in among the shorter dark. He had a certain stature to his walk. She couldn't say exactly how tall he was, slightly taller than Cousin Christopher. To her everything was tall anyway—even table, shoe and chair.

The Mild One must have known immediately that Beatrice was not a child. By her clothes and her voice both, he must have known it. She was always careful to dress like an adult, in order to avoid embarrassment. After he came to know her, he was careful not to make her feel like the others did—like an iguana skewered to a lapel with a yellow rhinestone pin.

When she first saw him, The Mild One was dragging an immense net from the side of the boat. Again and again he ducked under the boom as the boat came about, his chest bare and tan and lean above his raggedy white pants.

She knew in an instant that he could do anything to her that he preferred. Even at a great distance, she knew it the moment he looked into her face. In the same moment, she sensed that he would not. He did not stare; he merely looked. He looked into her, not at her, and it was the easiest feeling—as if she had just been slipped into a hot bath. From the shore, she could feel comfort the moment his gaze locked onto hers.

When she met The Mild One, also called The Desolate, she was all of these things: brief, broken, completely without faith even in seasonal rain and the passing of time. His stare was not about her size. Although he looked straight through her the moment he saw her, it was not horror in his eyes. Of one thing she was certain: it was not idolatry to idolize a saint. The Mild One that day held an empty net and with no small effort pulled it in—again and again.

She called out to him, "Excuse me, Sir—there's no fruitful fishing to be done in that pond—"

Beatrice, a remarkably smaller person, called out again to the stranger in the boat: "I don't mean to disillusion you—I'm sorry to say—That's a man-made pond, and they haven't stocked it yet."

Even before he answered, his face displayed a significant self-confidence. The afternoon light rippled around him on the lake. She did not sigh when she saw him, as others have since said of themselves.

She had always found the extraordinary to be appealing, unlike many of her neighbors who were afraid of anything different from themselves. Granted, some were a little more curious than others; they were gifted. She didn't know why.

"Sir—I could direct you further along if you like—toward a better place. Of course, you would have to move your boat. But—I don't see your trailer here?"

The high, grainy register of his voice burst out of his throat: "Little one, I'm not attempting real fish here—"

She raised her hand to rest it on the shoulder of her Great Dane. Already Gustaaf Glee craned his spotted neck toward the boat. "Oh," she said disappointedly.

"I'm only fetching the imaginary ones—"

No sooner had his voice called out to her than her dog began to sneer and bark. Then suddenly the beast pulled completely away from her, sprang into the water, and began his canine churning toward the little craft.

"Come back at once, Gustaaf," she cried. "Gustaaf Glee,

come back."

"What does he want?" came the shocked voice from beside the sail. The eyes in The Mild One's head looked like two black holes, side by side, burned into cloth.

Already Gustaaf Glee thrust his dripping grey muzzle over the narrow coning of the boat. His ears sat up in two, wet, black peaks on his head. Over the gunwale, his long front legs and whole grey body arched in one motion, his back feet scrabbling at the hull. Wildly, back and forth, the tiny red vessel rocked under the weight of the climbing dog as The Mildly Desolate Man tried to make way for him.

Already the man flung down his nets and let loose the flapping sail. Already he backed toward the starboard side to balance the weight of her ascending dog. Then he shouted toward her, his golden eyebrows darting up on his head. A gentle concern lined his face. "What does the puppy want, Little One?"

Gustaaf's dark wet body hung half in, half out. His back legs continued to scrape and churn. The Mild One leaned forward for a second to pull him in. "Is he in trouble, do you think?" No sooner had the man extended his hands than Gustaaf Glee lunged at him, savagely. A red liquid like a salamander burst across the stranger's palm.

"Oh no! No biting! Mr. Glee!"

The Mild One sucked intently on his fist; now he held it bleeding against his naked breast, a violet stream ran down his side. Now he pinched the hand under his powerful arm. Now he removed it again from his mouth. "Why did he do it, Little One?" he asked in anguish. "Did you ask him to do that to me?"

Perhaps her dog had been startled by the tenderness of that voice, a voice that was obviously never meant to feel or speak of pain. Before she could answer from the shore, Gustaaf Glee sprang into the water again.

"I don't know!" she cried in disbelief, staring at what her dog had done to him. "He's never bitten anyone before. I don't know what aggravated him! Maybe—?" she ventured. "And, I don't mean to be too critical, Sir—I'm not saying it's so, you understand—But maybe—It might have been your height."

The Mild One looked at Beatrice with pained astonishment. His handsome lip curled in his face. "Your pet's name is Glee, you said? The dog's name is Glee? What do you know of Glee, Little One? Reconsider your life."

THIRTY-FIRST DAY

Gustaaf Glee Goes Fishing

She would like to have been able to say that she was chivalrous in some way, that she went to The Mild One's aid, after her dog had grown so enticed that he had bitten him, but she could not. She was so frightened by the passions the ghostly man had aroused in her that she did what she would do if she herself had been the one assailed by a stranger and an immense dog on the very same day. When her drenched darling knelt down beside her, she climbed onto his back and off they rode, leaving The Mild One like a skeleton with hollow sockets staring after her. Looking back on it that night, she looked at it slightly differently. The man had not looked through her that time; he had stared at her as though he had been accosted by the Four Horsemen of the Apocalypse, a scene, almost certainly, that he had never once thought to approximate in his life.

THIRTY-TWO

Dog Bites Man

Six or seven weeks seemed to have passed in one night of reflection, and in that night her stomach turned into a stone and the stone itself was hammered into a pestle and then into a mortar with a hammer pounding it. The Immense Grandmère also passed on, unbeknownst to Beatrice, while she was dreaming again, of what might be. Long before morning, the dream as well as the leaves had begun to turn; the air was full of wind-borne red and yellow leaflets from the Great Beyond. She fancied herself in a grocery, collecting articles for her family's needs, standing on the upturned crate Rutherford Wilson always said he would provide for her, if she would only get out of bed. She held the butcher's hand and listened to the many worries of his family life. His worst travail in recent months had been the departure and loss of his beloved son. The boy had run off and been lost wandering homeless in a desert far west of where he lived. In her starved dream it was just as the butcher had described:

She stood on tiptoes atop the crate Rutherford Wilson

had turned over for her, staring over the shiny steel and glass meat counter, pointing at a sturdy-looking brisket of beef. "That one, please," she was saying in a vigorous voice of unprecedented confidence. What glory it was, she saw now, to stand up independently and transport oneself about in daily life.

Just then, the bell in front announced that someone had gained access to the butcher's emporium. Inside the door, The Mild One stood just beside the bags of potato crisps and plump fresh rounds of peasant bread. Under his white sports jacket, bound up in a sling, he carried his right arm against his blue-striped shirt. Those startling white adhesive tapes around his hand where Gustaaf Glee had bitten him, struck her, oddly enough, as being no less severe than the shroudlike dress in which she had, on a regrettable day, had her own gaunt body dressed. Suddenly The Mild One turned around and spied her standing in front of the fish counter in the act of staring at him! Immediately out he went again, his yellow-brown hair tied back in a ponytail with an elastic band.

"Excuse me," she cried, running after his long stride. "Excuse me, please. Couldn't we have a word?" Then he looked right through her! With those piercing eyes!

"Little One," he said. "Where is your dog?"

"Oh, please don't worry," she begged. "I've tied him to the barber pole out in front of the next store. He won't molest you any more."

No sooner had she said these words than she heard a yelping Gustaaf Glee come skittering up the street. The broken knot at the end of his leash cut a streak in the dirt, as he made straight for the man she had just consoled. Out from the curb in front of her, the skinny man leapt; and down the hill they ran. The thin man in the white linen suit had become a mote in the eye of the street with her own kindhearted dog a mere streak of debris lunging after him. She did not know what glowed more—the light off The Mild Man's thick gold hair, or the profile of her darling pet's extravagantly clean, white teeth—as the two of them ran round the large painted boulder that marked the final curve at the end of town. There the strong current of the river to this day must take its first bend or overtake nearly all of Dwarf Ville's low habitats. There her dog, the man, and the river disappeared into the circumstances of the next county, Story County, a place where those of Dwarf Ville emphatically feared to tread.

THIRTY-THREE

Little Pancakes

In this thirty-third bead on the string, the memory fought with the dream as though both had been drugged. For the first time, her crib seemed vast. The hunger no longer meant harm to her. Realities from the recent past lurched forth as though they were torments in the present. The dwarf, barely breathing on her own, twitched and moaned. Her skin seemed to solidify around her skull in a porcelain cast.

In recent memory, it was all too real. Adam Baum had made a bid for her, and to be sure of it, he had sent the first payment of twenty dollars by post in a yellow payment envelope. A date was written on the corner and an appointed time, three days to the future, so The Beautiful Mother said. Not to worry, her mother said habitually, that would be enough time for a certain dwarf to get prepared—if they began at once.

The Beautiful Mother found herself confronted with an external ferocity she had known only once: when as a child she had decided to give a tomcat a bath. The little lady kicked and flailed about, screaming all too clearly that certain things she had been washing for years herself. Other parts had never been washed, she asserted, and were never meant to be cleaned. The Beautiful Mother would hear none of it until satisfied that she was thoroughly sponged. Only then did she leave her to "collect herself if she would not cooperate." So doing, Beatrice looked up to see the unkempt facade of Uncle Thibault leaning curiously over her basket. Nowhere has it been mentioned in literature, or in life, that staring directly up a pair of nostrils into the very nose hairs that inhabit such darkness is a tempting thing. Most certainly, it will not happen here. But, then Uncle Thibault had departed nearly as quickly as he'd arrived. From all corners of the house came the wriggling sound of Uncle Thibault's suspiration, and not another resonance could intervene.

THIRTY-FOUR

Sees White Leggings

In her creel, she opened one eye and peered through the latticework. Her skin felt as though it had turned to scales. The thought of Uncle Thibault had made her nauseous many times in the preceding hours. She saw that someone must have attended to her yet again, for she lay gasping in a small white dress with a cummerbund and knotted rose buds embroidered round the hem. White leggings stuck out from under it; and at the ends, as if by miracle, white leather ballet slippers encompassed both her feet like closely carved fins. When she turned her head she found that her hair tugged. It had been combed out in an array around her face, in order to fall over the basket edge under a wide-brimmed hat with what felt to be cloth flowers attached to it. Her hair was slightly damp and had been tied up to twin lighted floor lamps to more evenly be dried.

It was only Uncle Thibault's remembered voice that was haunting her when the drone of Adam Baum now arguing with her mother started seeping in. "I should be allowed," he was stating to her mother, "after such generous payment against the extensive mortgage I hold against your farm, to take Beatrice from this house whenever I choose."

It was Uncle Thibault's voice she recalled, cooing at her from the too recent past, and the memory of his acrid scent. It might have been worse, she told herself, her eyes welling up again and again. For she had only seen the candlestick waving above her and the unlit wick flicking at her again and again and then—once or twice—felt his fingertips before her mother came in and tucked her in and sent him out to check on a limousine that seemed to be turning around repeatedly in the lane. It could have been worse she told herself but she did not as yet know how.

"We were just now leaving, Mr. Baum," The Beautiful Mother's voice in the kitchen brightly said. "You be a good girl now, Bea," she called toward the back room where Beatrice lay. "Did you hear what I said?"

At the bedroom door, the one called Adam Baum appeared with an azure blue sport coat over his shoulders and his white sleeves rolled up in the heat. Against his chest, he bore an explosion of peonies in whites and pinks. Unlike Uncle Thibault's face, Mr. Baum was cleanly shaved, his wavy hair thick and clean and neatly combed. A gentle scent of lavender floated around him as he leaned down.

"Well now," Adam Baum said to her. "What have we here? What do we have right here in front of our face? My little honey lamb?" he asked. "Is it you? I've brought you some flowers. Do you like beautiful flowers?" he asked.

She nodded as he untied her hair from the lamp, picked her up and laid her on top of all the cool, soft peonies he'd put in her basket again. And then he undid her ballet slippers and removed her stockings, saying it was much too hot for such things.

"Will you take me home with you?" she suddenly cried. "Please, please—Will you please take me out of here? You're a kind man, I can see it in your face."

"Some day I will," he said. "I was planning to do just that. But your mother says you are too young to leave her and she would die of grief."

"Die of grief?" she cried. And then, she threw her arms around his arm and would not let go. "Please take me with you," she begged again.

"Let me see," he said. "Let me examine you and then we'll see."

With shrieks she met him and clawed him like a cat—even an animal small as a cat can leave some sign of protest—until morning came again and he went, tattered and triumphant. It is said that the crooked place in his nose is where she broke it herself with the corner of a silver frame. Then he left her and she was made to lie there contemplating further what it had been to have roughly known human flesh of an unspeakable nature.

THIRTY-FIVE

Opinion Dissenting

The following sunrise her mother arrived to stare her down, but to the surprise of both of them she gasped when she saw the shredded reality of her daughter's clothing on the floor and even cried when she saw her lying there on all the pummeled flowers. The dwarf's voice was raw from crying and although her mother was the cause of the torture she had endured, she called out for her again as though she had been no older than two or three years. "Mama, Mama," she cried. But her mother would not take her into her arms. She merely stood crying over her, her tears dripping down on Beatrice's belly and bent legs.

"Will you send me to the circus?" Beatrice cried. "Now that he hates me?"

The Beautiful Mother looked startled for a moment as if addressed in court. "No, my darling," she said. "He doesn't hate you. In fact he says he has begun to love you. What he does to you, they call love."

"It's not love!" she cried. "I'll never believe it's love!"

She could not turn over to truly weep and she could

barely raise her arms to cover her embarrassment.

Her mother spread a dishtowel over her. "There," she said. "There. There's one good thing—"

"What is it?" Beatrice sniffed. "What is the one good thing? We get to keep the farm?"

"Oh no," her mother said. "He can't promise anything like that quite yet, he said. But he said you can still see your admirers."

"They can still come for advice?"

"No," she said. "Not those admirers. The ones on the list. They can still make up enough money to pay for the farm during the day. He won't hold it against you if you have other callers. There are just—certain things he reserves for himself."

"Certain things?" she asked.

"You rest now," she said. "Don't worry your pretty head about them at so early a stage in your development. I won't call your Uncle Thibault to bathe you just today. I will bathe you up before anyone else comes and I will make it clear. Everyone now has new responsibilities." She went out then, but in a moment she was back. "There's just one more thing," The Beautiful Mother said. "I think now it may be important after all that you begin again to eat. I've put a call into Dr. Every. God willing, he can still find his way up the street."

That day was the first time her mother had ever called

Beatrice pretty; and, in spite of everything, Beatrice liked her saying it. Through all of this, Beatrice had a difficult time understanding the concept of forgiveness, though decidedly she tried hard enough.

MEREDITH STEINBACH

THIRTY-SIX

Types of Darkness

The day after the transaction with Adam Baum—on the thirty-sixth day of her fast for tolerance of foreshortened persons—the One called Cousin Christopher stood in her doorway. Doctor Every had declined to come without advanced payment. "Do you mind if I come in?" Cousin Christopher asked. She could barely see him; the room was so dark, the sunlight so bright behind him. Her Immense Grandmère lay on the table in her dark blue suit, a yellow bouquet in her folded hands.

"I am not so certain whether you should come in, Cousin Christopher," she said, "although I've been looking forward to it for such a very long time. Today my mind is nothing but a silhouette."

"Which kind of darkness is it?" he asked, becoming in the doorway nothing but an outline himself.

"I have begun to lose track of the source of it," she said. "I began in darkness so far back."

"Sometimes it is better to eat, sometimes it is not."

"Oh it's not hunger driving me down," she had to say. "I

hardly think of it anymore."

"Then what is it?"

"First it was Grandmère dying—they are burying her today. Now it's my twin brothers. They said I forced them to take the branches of trees. They said I made them beat me during the night."

"I see it's worked," he said. "But I suspect it's something more."

"I've done no such thing!" she wailed, sitting bolt upright against the wicker edge of her permanent domain. "I've never in my life stripped naked before a fire and had my brothers beat me. It's a deceitful and outrageous story they tell."

"I heard it myself by the gate," Cousin Christopher said.

At this, she began to cry in a sickening tone, like a beaten animal. "They're telling it to everyone? That one, too? And, you believed those boys?"

"Do you mind if I come in?" Cousin Christopher asked again from the distance he politely kept. "The door is a little small for me, and I'd rather sit beside your bed where I can comfort you out of this fast."

She merely nodded into her arms, as her sounds could not be stopped, it seemed, even by herself who was at the source of making them.

"I didn't mean I believed your brothers," Cousin Christopher announced beside the bed. "No one would believe those stories—unless they wanted to harm you of course, and then they might just as well make up their own stories. Being pure is no insurance against lies and deceit. Surely you know that is just a myth."

Her head bobbed up and down on her neck while her fingernails pressed in at the sides of her temples as if one way or another her skull would surely burst.

"They might as well have whipped you," Cousin Christopher said, "looking at the effect it had on you—the story I mean. You might as well have at least had the pleasure of the fire in front of you, and their attention, although not quite like that—. You needn't look at me that way.

"Well," he went on, "you are lying here in a state of utter dejection about it and about the state of the world, aren't you? Starving yourself to death. Those twins are the laughing stock of the world, and you give them the power to trouble you? You need to be stronger for yourself. Wouldn't it be better to revel in the absurd moment perhaps, than to abandon all those who need you, merely to rid yourself of the mention of the ridiculous? Tell me just how you made those big brutes whip you. You, so tiny and weak you can't rise out of a basket. Reputations are for politicians. The great have no need for votes. You could emulate a higher source."

"They did beat me with branches, but just one time, as a joke. It wasn't just a story."

"I know that," he said. "Everyone knows it."

"But it didn't hurt. And I didn't ask them to do it!" she keened.

"I know that, too. That is what makes this house a circus and not a church."

"A church?"

THIRTY-SEVEN

Vintage Wine

"*Now,*" *Cousin Christopher said,* smiling down at her on the next day when he came to visit. "I am going to take you to see something—"

"How? But how?" she cried. She thought she saw evil in his eyes. "I have never left this house since I was a tiny child! I'm afraid! I will die out there!"

"No, little one. I will take you out."

"But the doctor says the light will cause me to fail! He said so when I was a little girl. My skin will blister and turn to boils, that is what my mother says. It happened to her as a little child. I know what sores are, and pain. I already have them now, from lying in this bed."

Cousin Christopher stretched out his long hands. "Come along, Little One."

"But I will be alone out there. What if I fall down in the road and no one will pick me up."

"You forget, little one, that others will come to replace the ones you leave behind."

"I am afraid of them. Branches are one thing, but there

have been worse things in my life."

"I know, Little One. It is written all over your face. Come outside," Cousin Christopher repeated. "If you would be eaten here by wolves you may as well be eaten out there by pups."

And then to her horror, he tried to force a sugar cube between her lips. But she would have nothing to do with it.

THIRTY-EIGHT

Providential Acts

On the third day of his latest round of visits, already the Cousin had put his long hands in along the edges of the basket and begun to hoist her up. "And if you don't come along quietly," he laughed, "I might give you the extraordinary pleasure of being beaten out of doors—very gently, of course!" He laughed again whole-heartedly, at the absurdity of the thought, "By myself."

At which, she, a minuscule person, was struck dumb and ceased shrieking all together. "Have you brought it then?"

"What is that?" the Cousin asked.

"The fruit," she murmured.

Cousin Christopher pulled her long hair from down around her shoulders and held it behind her head. He held her out in front of him, over the vast currents of open air swimming about her legs. For some time she gazed into the uncanny brilliance of his mahogany eyes. "Have I brought what?" the Cousin asked again.

"Oh," she nodded meekly. "I see it now. They were imaginary fruits."

"You have been inside so long, without food, and imagining the world—" he was saying as he placed her on his shoulders. And for the first time she truly saw Grandmère who lay on the table in the bundle of flowers. It was the first time she had truly seen anyone dead. There was no motion at all. It was as though Grandmère were her own older version lying in a basket herself. The only part of the world she cared about lay before her there inert.

"I'm afraid you will find it disappointing when you see the world. What will not be disappointing to you is this fact: That which comes after is always new. You think it won't be, but it always is. Do you allow yourself to understand?"

On his shoulders, gripping the top of his hair with grief for Grandmère, and shaking with fear, she tried to change her mind. But her cousin had a firm grip on her ankles. "Duck down now," he said. "Or I will have to crawl to avoid knocking your head. And don't forget! Always hold tightly to my neck. Men sometimes lose their hair, you know; I'd rather not have that affliction to add to my life just yet. Duck down, Miss Bea! I have an absent-minded streak; you will have to count, in part, upon yourself. Fruit—" he said. "I do remember something vaguely about fruit. Have you waited a long time?"

When he stepped into the sunlight that she had not seen since her infant days, except in her book of dreams, she saw that in reality the road was even shorter than the highway she had imagined and the roses scattered in the ditch were less a brilliant red than a deep and even, pungent pink. She could smell the earth rising up through the stems and thorns. A bumblebee became a small and delightfully textured and irksome thing. And it's bottom was not the fuzzy part that she recalled. As they went along, the road was black—with dampness he said. What a joy to have had a little rain in the midst of such a drought. The sky grew more white than blue as they made their exodus. The fertile hills rolled in yellow, furry waves of wheat into the day. She could not understand it. She had expected there to be a drought at the door, and the great flood beyond. Her mother had said she was selling her because of the Great Drought at their door, but she could see no sign of it on their property.

Beside the lane had developed a queue of hunched familiar persons in many shapes, all in squalid, brown hats; they waited down the shortest road and through the wire mesh gate. Past the white flowered hedge and up the distant bluff of wet clay and shaggy wiglike weeds, the filament of humanity stretched on—

"But, Cousin!" she cried as the Cousin strode, carrying her past the line. The formation, and in it many familiar faces, turned to stare at her where she perched on his shoulder like a parrot. Saddened and dumfounded, the crowd turned as they went past. "Cousin, it's me they are calling on—I recognize them; they have come for my advice!"

"Don't worry so, Cousin," he pointed out. "We will greet the latecomers, never fear. They are at the end of the line and are surely more in need of you than those who had the wherewithal to be early at the front."

But! He did not stop until long after he had passed the last one of them! Some time after that, the Cousin came to a complete rest and jockeyed her from his shoulder.

"Where are we going?" she asked. "Are we stopping here?"

He set her in the center of the road. "Walk," he said.

"Are you tired?"

"No, I rarely tire. Walk."

"I can't walk." Her legs splayed awkwardly in front of her as she fell on the perplexing dirt. "Even in my dreams, I ride—and that is on my Great Dane."

"As a little child, you once walked, I've seen it in my dreams," said Cousin Christopher. "You are not the only one with dreams. Walk again." And he walked away.

So quickly it happened. Before she knew it, she sat bawling in the road as he walked completely away from her. Surely he would come back to her, in a moment anyway, she thought.

The land stretched out in every direction, completely flat now, the sky falling in on her. In the distance she heard the delayed sound of the pick-ax breaking through the rectangular surface of dirt and her Immense Grandmère falling endlessly into it. She also heard the sound of her mother calling out, as she sold the funeral wreath: "Flowers for sale, two stems for a dollar, six for eight."

As her grandmother was buried, she, a little lady, lay on her belly, wailing into the coal black and drying earth. She sprawled on her back, and then she sat up and screamed into the sky until she fell asleep. Her head lolled on her chest as though she had broken her neck. In this position she woke, thinking perhaps mercifully an automobile would come dragging its exhaust pipes out the back end and run over her as had happened to The Limping Woman.

"Come back," she whimpered after the departed, distant relative. "I trusted you—I don't know where I am. I've never been outside. Please, oh please, come back?"

THIRTY-NINE

Days & Nights

Only when she opened her eyes did she realize that she was not entirely alone; an angry line of her penitents had turned around and was coming her way. A panic seized her. She would go back to the house where she felt safe. "Thibault!" she screamed. "Come help me, Uncle Thibault! Come help me! I don't know where I am." She lay down and sat up again, and then lay down. They were almost upon her now, she thought; but they were still there at a distance in their perpetual line approaching along the horizon. They chanted something as they came.

Mad thoughts came to her. She would stand up and throw herself under whatever car that eventually passed. And then she began to laugh. It would be too difficult to stand and throw herself. If she were actually to stand up enough for that, she thought, she might as well go away and see what she could see and, failing to stand, she might just as well drag her sticks along the dirty road in the direction in which Cousin Christopher had gone.

On and on her would-be callers came in their long

incessant line, ever approaching now, growing quite tall each one of them yet in the distance. "Double-dealer! Impostor!" they cried towering toward her. "Deserter! Low-life wench! You have left the sanctity of your own home!"

Along the rutted road that wound out in front of her, she crawled along on her belly, her little legs flung out behind her, aided only by a pair of very fine cast-off twigs.

FORTY

One Who Remained

On the road between one point and the next, someone known as The Cousin paced back and forth. Already Cousin Christopher had found the markings in the gravel where she must have dragged herself along using something like a ratchet. Holes were punctured in the earth where, he could clearly see, she had repeatedly dug her two sticks in, working them like rungs to a perpetual ladder, pulling herself up with her hands and then again and again pulling the pointed sticks out, driving them in, resetting her hands and jockeying herself upward, toward the opposite peaked edge of the road and out of traffic.

Even more obvious was the trough where the trunk of her slight body had burrowed through the surface gravel, and then the curious snakelike swerving where her feet had followed, dragged in tandem on their steel-capped ballerina points. And there! "Oh no!" he cried. In the ditch the grass had been matted down around a small mattress she had woven of reeds and padded with exploded milkweed pods.

"But, I only left her for a moment! There wasn't a car in

sight for miles and miles!" The Cousin grieved inconsolably. "Why oh why didn't I see her leaving?"

Now in this territory, it was true, anyone who wasn't completely blind and was at least two feet tall during the fallow seasons of the year could see to the horizon in any direction. The only interruptions consisted of two red barns and three distant white farm houses that were far too small for consideration, separated as they were by miles and miles of rolling plains, a silo there, an animal sty, a windmill here, the corrugated tin roof of Adam Baum's Egg Factory and the intimidating brick towers of his accompanying manse. All appeared in that northwest quadrant of the county. And there, too, were six toy hemlocks. But for those protuberances, it was open country. There seemed to be nothing at all behind which anyone, even a dwarf, might have hidden.

It was true, Cousin Christopher pondered, that there were two villages just on opposite sides of what the Cousin could observe with his beautiful mahogany-colored eyes, even at his more than extraordinary and yet increasing height, which pressed now well on past seven feet ten, and an edging upward quarter inch. "But," he raised his arms overhead as if to signal some imaginary crop duster, "it was only a second ago I left her! And there wasn't anyone at all in sight!" So he whinnied to himself. He did so despise himself when whinnying.

Over the tracings of her brief and miraculously rapid journey, in the bare spot her body had unearthed in a jet black stripe through the sharp gravel, Cousin Christopher discerned the overlaying tracks of a vehicle—which must have headed just as rapidly as she had, in one direction or the other.

Which direction it was, Cousin Christopher, not a detective, could not readily discover. The car tracks overrode her snakelike wriggle in the gravel.

Not unlike a man in an hallucination, staggering diagonally across the landscape, over the edge of which land lay a similarly confused continent, he traversed more of the same endless prairie grass, toward every point of the compass, reviewing the sad but simple scene that had detained him during which time she, a lady, seemed to have disappeared from the road and the planet all together. Her Cousin Christopher could not forget her stricken look when he had refused in that luckless moment to touch her tiny forehead for luck. He could not forget her faithful presence as he carried her, her hands painfully clutching and tugging at the lengths of his hair, the solidity of her torso as it had rested in a nearly radiant heat so briefly around his neck and shoulders. He stumbled then, too alone, rising to the challenge, continuing to call out dwarf names and their even fonder diminutives.

But—he swore it to himself in the way of excuses—he

had not lost concentration on her dwarfish whereabouts for longer than a fraction of one second, had he? He had merely chased the red poppy-like butterfly around the field a time or two, engrossed in its wee speech. He had never heard such a creature speak so clearly. The mantra of the hummingbird had, until then, been the most entrancing, too. He shook his head repeatedly.

By that time, his dwarf lady could have been anywhere in several counties—as well he knew—now that she had been picked up by a wide-tired vehicle.

She might even be in the traveling circus, he thought with building horror, or in the contortionists' menagerie that had started up in Aplington.

Or, she might be being held captive in the convent run by Carmelites, or strung up from the basketball hoop in the rival Story County Public School Gymnasium, or unnecessarily enrolled in sewing lessons at the Orange Tulip Orphanage, or making paper wallets in the Winston County jail, or indeed! chopping onions in a restaurant of ill repute, not that by now it would matter, or swinging in a birdcage in the famous antique shop that boasted the stuffed two-headed cow, surely they might have an unhealthy interest in a dwarf. She might even have been stuffed by now! No, that thought was too much even for the mild-mannered Cousin Christopher. He put it out of his head very quickly. Surely she was being held captive in some private home with a decent tea set or by an extreme religious sect which might even at that moment be converting her to a life of guilty views.

Held for ransom, or not for ransom, she was not the type, try as she might, to be able to resist nearly anything philosophical, or so Cousin Christopher believed. She would make the best of anything that came her way; it was the way she had survived. In any one of a thousand red barns or peeling turkey sheds or metal pig sties, on any one of a hundred-thousand oblong acreages, before that endless graph paper of a landscape that he had thrown her out upon, she might be crawling toward her new horizons, doomed. He was trying to think positively now. But, as he hurried around the bend of the new drive-through Watch It Zoo, live tigers appeared near Lake Marion. Yes, if she had been lucky, the Plain Tree Indian Reservation might have taken pity and forced food down her throat. Yes, he had meant to do it himself in just those very few moments—by enticing her, not forcing her, of course. A terrible thought overcame him: The Now Helpless Dwarf might merely have starved to death, alone, and been carried off by carrion, without any to record or even care about the last air-borne moments of her tiny husk.

Cousin Christopher felt a shiver start to run through the center of his spine in an increasingly pulsing rivulet. Even worse, she whom he had promised to rescue might have been picked up by Adam Baum and forced into his agro-economic scene of imprisoned chickens and their local indentured souls.

No, the track he had discovered in the dust was not too large to be that of Adam Baum's miniature sports vehicle with the outrigged high-riding, specially ordered snow tires, the one which he himself found so despicable with its Glorious Rooster embossed in the white leather of each bucket seat. It was in that direction then, that Cousin Christopher ran—if not for triumph, then for hope, and if not for hope then for consolation and good cheer if even from his enemies— as fast as ever he had run, toward the contemptible Adam Baum Egg Factory with its nightly lit, neon sign:

FERTILE EGGS CANDLED,
IF YOU PLEASE

If Adam Baum did not already have her, then surely Adam Baum might have an interest in finding her, and surely Adam Baum would have the means.

"If only," Cousin Christopher prayed, "If only she hasn't gone and starved herself to death."

But, already Adam Baum lay at her feet, staring up into her delectable face.

FORTY-ONE

Detour to Oblivion

So it was, on the afternoon of the forty-first day of her intended Eight-Day Fast to Oblivion that she awoke with a jolt, weighing in, she guessed, at twenty-four and one quarter pounds, but on an unfamiliar sofa. It had seemed like a dream to her: the transit from her nearly life-long basket, out her front door, across her yard, on the shoulders of the one called Cousin Christopher, only to be set down in the road again on the hottest day of the year, and without a pen or pencil, or even the Book of Dreams in which to write it down.

As she remembered it, she had clambered for several hours up a small ditch and then she fell to rest in a stand of milkweed shoots and thorny roses, which were most fortunately in full pink bloom. After a time, perhaps from lack of food and water, perhaps from other stressful incidents, the world, as she had never known it, began to spin around the conjunction of her nostrils. A large white piece of sheep's wool appeared above her in the bluest sky. The fuzz funneled downward like the white tail-tip of an angry yellow sky, turned to tornado. In tighter and tighter circles, it pivoted, followed by a bit of milkweed fluff and a halo of bright red thorny rose flames, swirling giddily at the edge, until finally in agony she herself had been sucked into the whirling vortex of her vertigo and plunged to the deepest bottom of the pit where she found herself face down and clinging to something soft.

Dark green as a cucumber rind, the velvet sofa lay with shiny, light green acorns of silk poking ever so slightly out of the nap—rather scratchily. Yet, the ceiling did not whirl. Nor now did the floor as she turned once again onto her belly. This might be effective, she had read, in avoiding further dizziness such as was wont to accompany the last stages of a hunger strike.

Her gaze ventured over the edge of the upholstery and into the surrounding topography of the room. The carpet stretched out olive and pink patterned toward an alien, white stone hearth. In front of the empty fireplace a substantial cat reclined, cleaning its long grey fur from top to tail. The cat was so grey, she began to notice, that it was almost blue; and under its blue fur, its muscles rippled like tiny waving fish. From the sofa, Beatrice could hear the rasping triangle of the cat's pink tongue combing out its long, blue, individual hairs, up and up again along its inner foreleg.

The cat had blue eyes as all babies had, or so she had been told since she herself was an infant learning to walk;

and in the cat's blue eyes, she, the perpetual infant now, found her brief allegiance. She had read of gigantic cats in zoos but there had been few close up pictures of housecats, since they were seemingly too normal for general interest. She had read, though, of one striped one that was bent on smiling and disappearing while it talked.

Her own arm hovered before her then in mid-air; her cheek rested heavily on the furnishing. A fragment of lace seemed to hang down over her wrist and, perhaps a nightgown whisked before the fan at the backs of her legs. She felt the bulk of a blanket, too, that some unknown individual had settled over her. A heavy chair had been pushed up to the sofa to keep her from rolling to the floor, on the chance, she supposed, that she should have a nightmare, or make a sudden move toward anything in particular while she was still asleep.

Somewhere in the unfamiliar chamber, a mouse chewed its way into a volume of *Caesar's Gaelic Wars*, taking out a few moments here and there to piece together strategies. The clock ticked just as predictably as all good clocks do. The sheer, white curtain drifted back and forth and tarried on the breeze. At some distance in the seemingly enormous house, a radio introduced Mozart in an undulating airwaved utterance. Static ran in and out, over-riding the accompaniment. A radiographic squeal lacerated her thoughts as the dial was shifted suddenly and then was moved to a more audible point.

She drifted in and out. Each time, as she gravitated toward sleep and startled awake, another facet of the parlor came to her: one dime stood on its end in a crack directly between the carpet and the hearth. The legs of a rosewood piano partially obscured her view of the striped room. A man's thin pant-legs crossed at the ankles in front of the lion's paw feet of a white wing chair. From above, reeled a piece of yarn that drooped and rose and rose again and seemed to tuck itself into a tall wicker basket. A thin metallic clicking entered invariably into the scene.

The cat had not moved, nor seemed inclined to accept any provocation toward that end, but for its steady bathing of its parts. Occasionally the enormous blue feline would stop to study Beatrice where she lay as though drugged. She knew it, too, as surely as if the cat had spoken: 'That dwarf,' the excellent cat was thinking, 'that dwarf is certainly too large to be any decent kind of baby. Stringy it is, and the belly is swollen with hunger. Alas, alas,' the cat was saying out loud to itself, 'there's not much meat.' The cat studied the dark pads of its paws, extending and retracting its claws, considering the prospects. 'Now there's the pity,' the cat was thinking nearly aloud.

With a start she awoke yet again to the back of a man's suit lurching, and the fat blue cat arching gracefully of its own volition in mid air. Its translucent foreclaws attached themselves then, as if with glue, near the bottom curtain edge. With a thump, the cat hit the wall, the draperies collapsed, and out from under the sheers fell the doomed rodent.

"You, Balderdash," a man's voice said calmly, "You must be ravenous. You didn't even take time to be playful with it." He leaned over the victim with his handkerchief. "Why, you've swallowed the head in one bite, Balderdash, my little greedy guts! This year you'll not be needing any spring training before your hunts."

FORTY-TWO

So Very Many Stripes

There are many kinds of deprivation: deprivation of air, water, love, comfort, and shelter; lack of physical affection, movement, recognition, education, meaningful society, too, can be lethal. And then, there is the question of the source of all these impositions. There was something else, Beatrice thought, could that be it? There was a question somewhere between mirage and reality. A question of the sauce, she thought, horrified, would it even be worth mentioning?

Staring at the center of a carpet that itself had been partially eaten——though not by herself but by ravenous moths, or so she hoped—she woke with a hunger gripping her intestines.

I am truly in a darkened frame of mind, she thought. Sainthood danced about the room on a skateboard of a reverie.

I have no need of mind at all just now, she thought. What need for thinking without food, and who needs it? In one stroke, she had erased two of life's necessities.

If someone would stick all these dust motes together, we might provide a proper burial for this wretched dwarf, she said to herself in a voice dwarfing her mother's. The dwarf laughed hysterically. We might apply a mustard plaster to the situation! she said in her grandmother's voice. Or was it Doctor Every's? She was losing her bearings.

Fans whirred, blue cat bathes, grey flannel man crosses narrow knees, yellow yarn reels down the long white hallway and into its own likelihood.

FORTY-THREE

Astonishing Evidence

She had turned in her sleep. The satin quilt slipped from her greatly swollen belly. Her other eye sprang open, anxious as a bug. It was not merely one neglected tray that lay cluttered before her now. She forcibly squeezed shut her eyes and dozed. Again, she awoke with a jolt, stared at the knees crossing near the alien settee, uncrossing themselves and crossing again as she lay strangely clad in hitherto unseen nighttime attire. A flowered shawl and an Indian blanket had been again thrown over her back. In her belly was an inexplicable stone as though she had been reincarnated to this. Beside her! What horror! Could this be?

A sorrier sight could not have appeared beside a wasting, hunger-stricken dwarf even in a nightmarish segment of the Book of Dreams! Strewn across the center of the elegant carpet sprawled more than six empty juice cartons! Twenty or so mauled lemon slices, sixteen lime wedges, four deflated packets of honey-roasted peanuts, the torsos of four crackerjack boxes with their ends chewed up, three jumbo sized pushup cylinders devoid of orange sherbet, her favorite, nine gnawed down bones from rib-eye steaks, eighteen wrappers for absent, chocolate-coated, squishy yet ultra-crispy, marshmallow sandwiches, one root beer bottle drained with one plastic drinking straw half-devoured. Two watermelons had been seriously disemboweled right to their dark green rinds, four lemon meringue pie shells gutted, . . . How many people had dined, perhaps in her presence, as she slept ignorant of this paradise? And, with what lack of etiquette? Thready tidbits of licorice shoelaces draped themselves in a swoon over the last of the dozen tattered kernelless cobs of corn. The spent confetti of the missing kernels lay on a plate among an array of broccoli feather-dusters floating in a pool of aromatic garlic butter sauce. A bit of truffle lay smudged against a half-nibbled cheesecake wedge; one curl of radicchio topped one bone-white pyramid of poultry wings in a hardening lime-green ledge of gelatin.

Two spirals of carrot shavings coupled in a creamier spume, bore up the stem of one black maraschino cherry pit. Two industrial-sized, empty cans reeked strangely of maple syrup—their tin tops had been ripped out as though by mechanical scissors. Or, metal teeth. A can of whipping cream barely dribbled now; the contents of a sarsaparilla bottle had been sucked. Half of one hamburger bun mustard-streaked, one French fry broken in a subterfuge of orange barbeque salt, almond husks, walnut frills, six gnawed plum pits, vacant Dwarf-sized Vienna sausage cans, and pistachio hulls drifted in waves across the carpet. . . There on the hardwood, not far from her, lay the telltale story of a shrimp cocktail tail and the end of a baguette. "What on earth is that?" she called out.

The blue cat bounded away as she moaned; then a short bark of laughter dominated the room. The legs had come unglued again, seemed to step forward nearer to her, the unseen torso rested firmly on the pin-striped ankles—by extension from the unseen hips. She felt too sickly now to lift her head. Across the room, the newspaper came down to rest on the side of one knee.

"What was it, you mean?" a familiar voice answered.

"I didn't do it!" she claimed. "I didn't eat a bit of it. I couldn't have."

"I wouldn't want to disillusion a fine lady before she has even risen from her nap. But let me put it to you gently: Even my cat didn't help."

"But I'm fasting toward something good. I'm on the forty-third day!" Her fingers, she realized then, were a cornucopia of incriminating scents.

"Thirty-ninth day, the newspaper said. But, if you say that's fasting, I'm a poor man. A poor, poor man living on an egg ranch, without even one chicken," he chortled. "This is my egg farm, you must have realized."

"What do you mean thirty nine!"

Adam Baum leaned in her direction, beaming widely. And so it was, after she had counted and recounted. She saw that somewhere very lately, while she was in a faint of hunger, she had thought a whole week to have passed when it had only been one hour. And now she, quite alone, had thrown away all sense of responsibility and had been responsible for cramming down goose with stuffing, candied yams, young asparagus tips, and cranberry jellies along with the origins of every remnant laid out before her, and on a formerly spotless carpet. Her little nightgown resembled a very clumsy chef's apron.

Adam Baum reached up and pulled the rope to the antiquated bell. A heavily aproned girl responded with a pink bottle. "There now," the farm girl said. "There now, we'd better have us some of this magic potion or we are most certainly going to hurk all over Mister Baum's brand new imported Aubusson. Quick now! Get hold of yourself, lassie! You've made a colossal mess, already crawling about from course to course, and for such a small girl! I think you surely should be sainted for this in the Book of the Most Remarkable! LITTLEST WOMAN IN THE WORLD EATS BIGGEST MEAL ON EARTH! What do you think? I plan to write it in my diary—unless you would like the honors yourself?"

FORTY-FOUOR

Change of Guard

When the county sheriff's crew was hoisting the littlest saint, a quite exquisite and ladylike little dwarf—even for a dwarf, the papers said, she was minute-—away to the county jailhouse, it looked to nearly all the bystanding county residents as though the completely wrong perpetrator had been placed under arrest. In the ambulance lay a seething Adam Baum, detested egg meister, sole ruination of their grandparents' regal grandparents' grandparents' dignified names. Away, in chains, the saddened sheriffs and their deputies carried the surrounded little dwarf, while long side the road, stumbling into the scene, The Mild One began to weep, and then he hurried off again at the sight of a set of seemingly ravenous canine police, there to watch again as his distant little cousin was being driven away from his sweetly swaying field of wheat.

Cousin Christopher leapt up and began to emit an unearthly howl. He plucked his hair in lamentation and ran alongside the retreating car. "If only you had kept your faith in me, Bea, and hadn't run away! You wouldn't have lost your brand new freedom!"

Beatrice lifted her eyes to see him. "I haven't lost my faith in you," she said. "Who knows what miracles this may bring! Besides, where were you?"

"But! You nearly killed someone!" Cousin Christopher shouted.

"I would never mean to kill anyone," she said meekly as the car slowed to make way for the crowd.

"But, of all people to shoot. They'll likely give you life imprisonment for taking the littlest nail off of Adam Baum's foot, to say nothing of what must have happened to his best shoes."

She admitted that she had looked upon her rescuer with the ungrateful face of an unadorned skillet. "Who knew such a little wound could bleed so profusely?"

"Bea! Bea! Bumble Bee," the Cousin called, looking down from his great height into the uniformed group gathering around them.

"Please don't despair, Cousin Christopher—" she called out as the youngest deputy tried to push him aside. "I don't hold your tardiness against you—And, on that other little matter, dear sir, it wasn't truly attempted liquidation. Truly, I merely aimed at his little toe and the pistol shot at it. That is all I have to say. I presume that you will have many chances to sit around with me and visit, I do hope. Perhaps I will be out by morning light—"

"But, who will believe you are so good a shot as to be able to shoot off his little toenail on purpose?" Cousin Christopher called as he followed the moving car along, plunging now through the flower beds and along the ditch. "The Egg Man went into shock just at the sound of it. It looks like he might die!"

"Oh, it wasn't all that hard, and such men never die," Beatrice countered. "Besides, I didn't harm his shoes. He had just taken them off, along with his socks. I had to defend myself, didn't I? Keep your chin up, Christopher!"

RETROSPECTIVE

Her Portrait in Miniature

And so, Beatrice, a former faster, currently a prison inmate and avid correspondent, soon found that she had begun to gain strength and also stature on prison life and fodder. Oddly enough, it was as though she finally had been allowed to go to school, to church, and to the millinery. Even the butcher's, the library and town council meetings seemed to be included in her vacation package. And even, can you believe it?, she was almost immediately admitted to a kind of country club of the permanently imprisoned. Physical therapy for her multitude of aches and pains and lessons in massage led her to join the prison hospital auxiliary! Before long, she had collected a steadfast following among the petty enthusiasts of armed robbery, the drunkards, irate cuckolds, cattle rustlers, and tax evasionists, and also those who had carried pickets for numerous reasons in front of the Winston County constabulary. Her ministry, and what appeared to be her everlasting penance for attempted murder, began to gain attention from the media.

Not surprisingly, Beatrice's teachings soon included

the need for a renewed commitment to the peaceful life, no matter how microscopic, and to everyday, large, and undersized philanthropy. She felt particularly refreshed when the movement gathered backing on death row where even the blameless had dubbed her their Littlest Saint, and in some townships: The Pious Mite Who Arrives Like Salt in Wounds Not Of Our Own Making. On the Outside, some began to dub her their Tiny Renovator of Locked Souls, or, occasionally, Our Saintly Child of Secure Units. All was not completely lost, she told her Cousin Christopher when he came for his Saturday consolation. After all, their penitentiary now appeared in many guidebooks so that tourists and pilgrims alike might more easily come to stand beneath the stone towers under an eddy of barbed wire and stare up longingly through the thorn-like shadows. Each day the crowds increased in their gatherings.

One day soon, Beatrice daily hopes and fears, Cousin Christopher will surely spring her loose. At night, when all are locked securely away from outside ills, the chant starts up, and then the rattling of the cups along the bars. In her prison cell, the Little One sits dead center of her bunk. Just below, her new life-long companion rises up respectfully on a stalwart elbow.

"I forget who's next," Beatrice announces. "Please remind me—"

The trinket moves from hand to hand, passing around

and beyond each iron dowel, comforted by every inmate.

The little present looks up at her with the smallest of frightened eyes.

"Tell us your stories," she tells the infant rodent. "Tell us how it was you came to be in such a predicament."

About the Author

Meredith Steinbach is the author of *Beata Rustica: The Tale of the Would-Be Saint*, *The Charmed Life of Flowers: Field Notes from Provence*, *The Birth of the World as We Know It; or, Teiresias*, *Zara*, *Here Lies The Water*, *Reliable Light*, one play and numerous short stories.

Prizes and honors have included 2013 Paris Book Festival First Prize/international general fiction category; 2012 New England Book Festival, Honorable Mention/general fiction category; Thomas J. Watson Institute Travel Grant for Research in France and Greece; the Bunting Fellowship of Radcliffe College at Harvard University; O. Henry Award for the Short Story; 100 Distinguished Stories, Best American Short Stories; National Endowment for the Arts Fellowship; Pushcart Prize for the Short Story; Rhode Island State Artists' Grants.

She lives in Rhode Island in a sea captain's cottage with her family and a spin-dancing corgi and a Great Pyrenees mountain dog. She is Professor of Literary Arts at Brown University.

From the Reviews,

THE CHARMED LIFE OF FLOWERS: FIELD NOTES FROM PROVENCE, a novel by Meredith Steinbach

THE CHARMED LIFE OF FLOWERS is award-winning novelist Meredith Steinbach's magical tale of camaraderie and delight in the face of adversity. Professor Steinbach reconsiders and reconstructs the components of an old-fashioned fairy tale in this modern day novel set off the beaten path in the vineyards and olive groves of Southern France. When Pearl Queneau, the little albino schoolteacher, seeks refuge in the village of St. X, even the plants and animals transcend their days as textbook entries and come to life for her. Here she falls in love with the proverbial Woodcutter and raises her son in an atmosphere of increasing tolerance and generosity---but for the ill will of a few miscreants who would try to cause them irreparable harm.

Reviews & Accolades:

Winner, 2013 Paris Book Festival, international general fiction category

Honorable Mention, 2013 New England Book Festival, general fiction category

CAROL LOEB SHLOSS: "This book is as improbable as it is delicious, as dark as it is full of rapture. Above all, it is a meditation on the delightful colors of all growing things: adolescent sons, surviving mothers, and the eels and hedgehogs and plane trees and flowers that inhabit the small villages of our imagination. An amazing read... so scary and yet so incantatory."

JOE W. HALDEMAN: "*The Charmed Life of Flowers* is a love-letter to Provence and to the lives that are intertwined there, animal kingdom and the vegetable one, as well as the charmed and charm-less humans who drift through and observe, and know a little. The writing is evocative and accurate and hard to put down."

THE BIRTH OF THE WORLD AS WE KNOW IT; OR, TEIRESIAS,
by Meredith Steinbach

"In her fourth book of fiction, award-winning American novelist Meredith Steinbach reimagines the life of the Greek seer Teiresias. Having outlived everyone he ever knew, the seer looks back at the most significant episodes in his life--a visit to the Delphic oracle, mediating arguments between Hera and Zeus, his experiences as both man and woman--as he confronts the traveler Odysseus in the Underworld. Narrated from shifting points of view with tremendous psychological acuity, Steinbach's novel intertwines time, event, and narrative."

Reviews:

Publisher's Weekly: "…a metaphysical tour de force. Steinbach's writing is as elegant as a neoclassical column."

St. Louis Post Dispatch: "Her latest work of fiction, *'The Birth of the World as We Know It,'* [is] a witty cross-breeding of Greek tragedy and contemporary fiction. Think James Joyce and Homer in a running conversation."

MARJORIE GARBER, Harvard University, Vice Versa: "I take the liberty of quoting at length because Steinbach's work is not as familiar as Eliot's or Joyce's, and also because Steinbach does something they do not. She imagines Teiresias in the moment that will answer the gods' question."

Chicago Tribune: "The source of the considerable strength of *Teiresias* resides not only in the vividness with which Steinbach imagines each event of her narrator's life, but in her willingness to let those episodes collect and cumulatively resonate in her reader's imagination… narrated with an extraordinary and just passion."

Harvard Review: "superbly orchestrated, ornate, convoluted retelling, one in which she has spiced up, ad-libbed, and otherwise domesticated, re-routed, authenticated, and tampered with the archetypes. Steinbach seems to be following no other voice than her own; the result is a shamanistic meditation on the telling of time, the telling of history."

Boston Review: "She is like Joyce, mingling an ironic undertone with sensuous descriptions of vintage cosmetics, sexual sporting, war, and grief. Plot is shiftily dispersed throughout the book, playfully revising the natural sequence of events, so that the novel reads rather like a long, accelerating prose poem borne forward by its rhythms."

ZARA, by Meredith Steinbach

"'Zara Montgomery has not had an easy time of it in this town,' the housekeeper tells us. In moments as close as dreams, as impersonal as newspaper accounts, Meredith Steinbach gives us the life of Zara Montgomery—the precocious only child of a successful Midwestern physician and a failed British lieder singer. In *Zara*, Steinbach has given us fiction as it was meant to be—exacting, compelling, and enduring. The lucidity of this writing, the intricate craft of her structural designs, the richness and humanity of her characters, all point toward Meredith Steinbach as a novelist of exceptional power."

Reviews:

JOHN HAWKES: "Rich, horrific, beautiful, *Zara* is about the life of a woman extraordinary in every way, and is written in prose as strong and fabulous as Zara herself. I could not admire more this profound and exhilarating novel."

HILMA WOLITZER: "Zara is a beautifully realized character whose story is constantly engaging and moving. Ms. Steinbach is gifted and nervy and her book is very accomplished."

BOSTON REVIEW: "She's a critic of myth who also chooses to re-dream and brilliantly reinvent it. In *Zara*, . . . she considers the challenge of heroism in an American setting."

Los Angeles Times Book Review: "Steinbach probes vulnerability, futility in a style interlaced with quality and power."

Chicago Tribune: "The completely written quality of *Zara* marks an author page by page discovering the giddy limits of her talent. . . . I doubt a finer first novel will be published this year."

Chicago Magazine: "A rare, invaluable prize."

Boston Magazine: "A masterpiece."

HERE LIES THE WATER
by Meredith Steinbach

"Steinbach's intense novel of a circle of friends in rural New England addresses the misunderstandings and lies that destroy people by depriving them of 'the human will to love and learn.'"

Reviews:

Hungry Mind Review: "There's far more metaphor in *Here Lies the Water* than plot or character. Let's read it like a poem. The descriptive language is remarkable. . . . We are sustained by loss, memory, and the order and beauty of art. . . . Steinbach's prose is opulent, musical, disconcerting."

The New York Times Book Review: "Meredith Steinbach would probably cringe at the comparison, but her second novel is the spookiest tale of life gone wrong in suburbia since Ira Levin's *Stepford Wives*... As these revelations mount, ... its gorgeous but sometimes soporific prose becomes its strength, for it makes the wallop that's packed at the end even more powerful."

RELIABLE LIGHT by Meredith Steinbach

"In this collection of seven stories, Steinbach again distinguishes herself as a writer of sensitivity and grace. The effect is of real voices and real situations, portrayed with scrupulous fidelity to human nature. In robustly simple and direct prose, Steinbach introduces characters who range from an old woman in a nursing home to a black doctor in a New England village. In 'To Be Sung on the Water,' a woman visiting her mother's grave with her sister and young nephew is dismayed to find it sunken and filled with water. The boy's question, 'Why is your mama sleeping in that little lake?' helps bring the protagonist to a moment of transcendent understanding. 'In Recent History' observes the people whose lives have been profoundly affected by one man's experience in Vietnam, which he is tragically compelled to recreate. In the aftermath, the narrator occasionally glimpses the man and thinks, 'How strange and painful to see his face, as if he had not one terrible secret moment in his heart.' Constructed with a quiet and effective craftsmanship, these tales range in tone from comic to tragic, displaying the diversity of Steinbach's interests and themes."

Reviews:

Publishers' Weekly: "In this collection of seven stories, Steinbach again distinguishes herself as a writer of sensitivity and grace."

The New York Times Book Review: "Meredith Steinbach has won both a Pushcart Prize and an O. Henry Award for short fiction, and it's easy to see why. At her best, she gives us what we want from stories: root emotion recognized through someone else's consciousness.

CPSIA information can be obtained at www.ICGtesting.com
Printed in the USA
BVOW11s1133070914

365818BV00010B/49/P